CW01083924

Spice

Spice Traders is my first novel. I'd always liked the idea of writing and am an avid reader. During the lockdowns of 2020 and 2021 I found myself with a lot more time on my hands. I got pen to paper, or fingers to the keyboard and here is the result.

I'd like to thank the following people whom without this project would never have been completed, my wife Michelle and my daughter Joanna. My sister and fellow author Ruth Brooks for her support, Steve Dunn for his proofreading and advice as well as my friends, family and social media connections for their encouragement. I hope you enjoy coming on this adventures with the Spice Traders.

All the best

Dan

Chapter One

It was about food. Well, the preservation of it. A rumour had led her to a food storage device here. Why it was in a crypt, she didn't know. Was it sacred? Galaxio's torch flame was their only light. A crisp breeze blew, and the torch flickered. Sounds of hurried feet clattered towards them, like a court martial army.

"May I remind you we need to be quick?" Galaxio said as she clicked the dial to the left.

"There!" Valentina said, stepping backwards. With a scrapping sound, the stone rolled away. Bile came into her throat as clicking sounds greeted them.

"I think there is something unpleasant in here," he said, holding his nose.

"Well, we won't be long."

"Don't count on it. Listen to them sharpening up their fangs!" Galaxio said.

"Give me the light, I wish to try something." After she received the torch, she waved it in the sound's direction, and the creatures recoiled. "Just as I thought, these are Midnight Spiders, sunlight kills them. If you wave the flame at them, they should stay way."

"Now that we are here, I do not wish my tombstone to read: eaten by spiders."

"To die that way would be terrible," she said

"Try not to scare me. Can we just get on with it?" The Passageway was tight; they had to squeeze against the stonework. The vermin were too large to follow. The crypt opened out into a larger area. The torch revealed an altar with a square item on it. Galaxio took out a tape measure and measured the object.

"It's 80cm x 50cm," he said.

"Okay, let's hope we can get it out of here."

They could hear crashing sounds from the other side of the wall. The room shook and dust fell on them.

"Look, up there!" Her servant pointed the flame in the direction she showed. There was a thin slither of sunshine beaming onto the ground, a ray of hope in the darkness. "Galaxio, hand me my bow." He passed her the weapon. She fired at the hole and the gap grew, but it wasn't big enough. She shot again, and the hole widened to fit a child through. Third time it was big enough. The crashing stopped, and the monsters appeared.

The lead animal landed with a thud and tried to flee, but it was too late. The sun had singed its skin and the air smelt of burnt hair. The helpless fiend turned to ash, no longer a threat. Its followers witnessed the scene and fled.

They fastened the rope around the device, and they hoisted it through the gap. Galaxio mounted the ledge and pushed the item clear of the hole. Valentina took his offered hand, and he pulled her up. She whistled for Zilli. Thirty seconds past and a gigantic eagle landed with a squawk. After clambering on its back, they secured the unit, and they flew to Tarnuz.

<u>Chapter Two</u>

With white fingers, he held on to the terracotta tiles. He couldn't see much through the blinds. Nadal, the king's vizier, weighed coins whilst talking to another man.

"These are superb quality," Nadal said.

"Excellent, I am glad you are happy with my workmanship. It is surprising how much is being used," the other the man replied. He had a voice as rough as sandpaper. Alessandro tripped on the roof plates and Nadal glared at him.

"It appears we have an intruder, get him," Nadal said. Alessandro slipped on the shingles and slid down the canopy to the ground. Four armed guards went after him. Passing a pottery seller, he rolled large earthen vessels, and two pursuers fell. Next, he came to a trader pulling a trolley loaded with wicker baskets. He vaulted this, but caught a basket, spilling its contents on the floor. A king cobra escaped, and a soldier got bitten. He raced past a washing line and flung it at his pursuers. He rushed around the corner and into the palace grounds. Running into the kitchen, his mum said hello.

"Are you okay, son? Please stop."

He stopped and faced her.

"I was being chased by Nadal's guards!"

"What have you done now?"

"I saw him talking to another man with a gruff voice. They were hatching some kind of a plan," He replied, catching his breath.

His mum had a shocked looked on her face. "Son, Nadal is always hatching plans." "We need a bit more to go on Alessandro," She said

"It's the truth!"

"We'll talk about this later. As you know, we have a meeting with the king," Vernu replied. They walked to the royal chamber.

The throne room walls were lined with gold mouldings depicting battles fought between man and beast. Oil paintings lit by candles portrayed royal ancestry. One was of King Stefano and Nadal as young princes. The King, their father and the Queen and the boys were dressed in Royal attire.

Gold chandeliers hung from the ceiling.

A maroon drape with gold triangles and a blue lining was held in place by two gold posts and fastened at the top with a large crown.

A painting of the Royal Coat Of Arms adorned the floor, a knight slaying a dragon. There were three red velvet carpeted steps that led to a modest throne, with a round back, cushioned with navy velvet and gold circle pattern on it.

Twelve guards stood to attention, facing each other. Their armour was gold, and they held lances. Six courtiers sat opposite each other on red velvet stools with gold legs. The head courtier introduced the king, and he took his seat, followed by Nadal, who scowled at Alessandro. Alessandro and his mother, Vernu, stood next to the naval Admiral Cilistinu and his daughter Valentina.

"I suspect you are wondering why I have called you here," King Stefano said, the black ringlets on his beard moved when he talked. "I am very disturbed. My rival, King Khalid of Birik is threatening to make war with Tarnuz, unless we cook him a special meal." "He claims his country is experiencing a famine." "If that is true, I hope he shares his food with his subjects."

"It's not a problem, my staff and I will be happy to make it for him," Vernu said.

"I have never doubted your food. It has always been of the highest standards, but Khalid has very particular ingredients. Here is the note." He handed the list to the vizier, who passed it to the chef.

"I am happy to source ingredients for you, but some of them are on hostile islands," she said, after reading the note.

"All of my resources I will make available to you," he stated as he leaned forward on his staff. His other hand stroked his beard. Nadal bent over and whispered something in his ear, knocking the King's crown and the King straightened it.

"I can't stand and watch this crook whisper lies to you, your highness. I am off!" Alessandro said and turned to leave, but the curved lance blades blocked his path.

"May I remind you, like your father before you, you are a trusted member of my royal team?" "I will dismiss you when I say so. Guards, you may put your lances away." The guards withdrew, and the room relaxed.

"Admiral Cilistinu, have you received all the provisions for the trip?"

"Yes, your majesty we have."

"Very good Valentina, is the cooling unit in place?"

"Yes, your highness, we have everything we need."

"Vernu, keep your son in check. He is a gifted warrior, but he has no manners."

"I will make sure he behaves himself, your majesty.

"I am pleased. You must succeed, Tarnuz is a small country and I do not wish to take up arm. Good luck. You may leave now," he said and clapped his hands.

The group said thank you, bowed and left.

"Follow them, the king said to Nadal. I don't trust that Alessandro."

Nadal smiled like a fox about to eat a rabbit.

"Your highness, I will leave right away."

After a thirty-minute ride, they dismounted and led their horses onto the ship. The Sibell was being loaded by the crew. Vernu strode up the gangplank and began ticking things off her checklist. Cilistinu pulled on ropes, checked the sails, the rudder and the captain's wheel. Everything seemed in order.

"You seem to be very thorough, Admiral Cilistinu, Vernu said.

"Call me Stinu, it's easier to say. You can call Valentina, Tina, too."

"Ah, fair enough. Alessandro answers to Ali too."

"Noted. Let's keep things simple!"

"Agreed," Vernu said, smiling.

And Stinu smiled too.

"You must have seen a lot of exotic countries. Why do you keep returning to tiny Tarnuz?" Vernu asked

"Tarnuz is the centre of the known world. Everything comes through here. We have a reputation for imports and exports. Everyone wants to trade with us and we are strategically placed, right in the centre of Remina. A man or woman needs a place they can call home and exotic islands may tempt with beauty, but there's nothing better than your own bed and Tarnuzian mead. Join me in the crow's nest and let's take a look. Ali, you should join us too." Stinu climbed the mast and Vernu and Ali followed. Stinu panned his telescope across the landscape.

The capital was built on a peninsula between two harbours. Baroque buildings made a grid with wide straight streets to allow the sea breeze to blow freely in summer. Invaders were a common threat, so the city was fortified, that being said, it had charm and character. Buildings had coloured awnings tied to posts and dwellings were brightly painted. Some had tasteful graffiti on the front, depicting people laughing, playing wind instruments and drinking wine. A butcher had various cuts of meat painted on the side of his establishment. A fish monger had fish painted on his shop. Seagulls patrolled the air looking for scraps. Children rolled dice against a wall and a linen trader steered his oxen and cart towards the market. Camel traders herded their beasts with sticks and the animals groaned as they moved. Fruit pickers yelled at children as they stole peaches and nectarines from heavy ladened trees. Traders in the market competed for business, each one tried to be louder than their neighbour. Fine cloth, wicker baskets, animals, scribes, fruit and veg, perfumes, and tinctures were all available at the right price, if you were prepared to haggle.

A mother with three small children greeted the baker at his stall. He smiled and gestured towards crusty loaves. She picked up two, and tried to pay, but a Birkrian soldier wrenched one of the loaves from her hand and gave it to the baker. He held up his index finger, gesturing one loaf only, and then he pointed at her and her family and the loaf in her hand, and then he pointed at the road leading out of the market. Before leaving she looked at the cobbled market floor, and then she gathered her children and left.

"That family may have to skip some meals this week," Stinu said, sighing

"What just happened?" Ali said, anxiously.

"Have a look at the bakers stall," Stinu replied, handing the telescope to him. Pointing the telescope at the stall, Ali saw the guards harassing the baker. One had a hand on the hilt of his sword, and the other guard yelled at the baker whilst he busied himself rearranging loaves and cakes with trembling hands.

"I need to do something about this," Ali said.

Stinu held him back, placing his hand on Ali's chest.

"Let me have a look, please?" the Admiral said.

Ali handed the telescope to him, reluctantly.

Stinu studied the perimeter of the market and watched as a mounted detachment of guards arrived, they dismounted and a captain barked orders to his troops.

"We can't get involved. There are too many of them," Stinu said collapsing his telescope.

"The pair of you had better crack on with your preparations," Stinu offered.

"He's right, let's go Ali," Vernu agreed.

"Oh, okay," Ali said, looking worried, and they both climbed down to the deck. When he was sure they had gone, Stinu opened his telescope again and trained it on the harbour.

Ships came to and fro on the emerald sea in the harbours announcing their arrival with bells. Dock workers hurriedly unloaded the vessels. A strange mixture of perfume, fish, fruit, spices and animal dung filled the air, made worse by the scorching sun. Pride and professionalism was gloriously displayed in Tarnuz.

It might be a small country, but it had plenty to offer and the traders knew it. Some would try and get the better of Tarnuzian good nature and easy going attitude, only to be greeted with a sharp blade to the throat. Negotiations quickly resumed and swords were sheathed.

***

Alessandro sharpened his Nimchar, and then he sharpened his Jambiya, his dagger. Some Jambiyas were made of rhino horns, but none of his father's weapons were crafted this way. Ali took a dim view too, and all of his Jambiyas were one hundred percent animal friendly. Some beasts needed to be slain, but rhinos weren't one of them. It had a crescent-shaped blade, and the emerald on the hilt flashed in the noonday sun. They left both weapons to him in his father's will. And they had served him well.

And he guarded them with his life. He then started sharpening the Nimchars and Jambiyas for the group. After he finished, he tested them on the fencing dummy. Everyone needed training. It's okay to fight alone, but even better if you have backup. After he had finished, he made his way below deck.

Nadal observed them from his ship with his fist raised in the air. He waited half an hour for the Sibell to become a small dot on the horizon, and then he lowered his arm and ordered his crew to give chase.

Valentina had her back to him. She wore a long red dress with matching tassels. A curly brown hair dropped into her eye. She tucked it back under her gold tiara. As Alessandro got closer, he saw some drawings with strange machinery on it. The top left corner read "Dyidian Horseless carriage."

"Why are you fascinated with the Dyidians?" He said.

"Well, where do I start? What interests you?"

"I like money. I want to be rich one day."

"They invented money. You name it, they probably discovered it."

"Wow! That's impressive. He said, widening his eyes. What happened to them? I don't think I have seen one."

"Some say a gigantic meteor killed them, others believe it was a plague and, my personal favourite, space invaders carried them away." Tina said.

"Ah, come on aliens, really? Anyway, they all sound like horrible deaths to me!"

"You can see why they appeal to me, can't you?"

"Yes, I can. You're not so bad for a nerd, you know. I feel like I learnt something!" Ali said, bluntly
"How did you convince the King to become an archaeologist?"

"I was expected to go into the navy. But the King is a just and noble monarch. I think it makes his job easier if a child sticks with tradition and follows their parents into the family business. He just signs a piece of scroll and the scholarship can begin. We had compelling evidence that he couldn't ignore, and when he saw that it would bring knowledge and knowledge brings power and wealth, he had his scribes draw up a unique scholarship for me."

"Besides, we live on an island in the middle of Remina, so sailing is involved, so I still had a lot to learn from my father. I think I was the first female to have unique scholarship tailored to my own chosen path."

"I don't think you were," Ali said, frowning.

"What makes you so sure," Tina replied, folding her arms and scowling at him.

"My mum was allowed to change careers after I was born and the King drew up a new scholarship for her."

"Oh I see. I didn't have a clue," "I just thought she was always the royal chef." She replied, with a sigh and then she unfolded her arms.

"No she had another career before. She won't tell me about it, so I gave up asking. I just know she worked with my father."

"Do you like studying books?" he asked her.

"Books can be dry," She said, straightening her back. The candle light caught her brown eyes. Excitement and adventure danced there, and he hoped his eyes said the same. "But when you see them in real life, it can astonish," She said.

"What about you Ali, did you try to pursue a different path to your father?" Tina enquired.

"No. From the moment I could walk I had a sword in my hand. I didn't feel nervous as my seventh birthday approached. I assumed I would follow in my father's footsteps. And what was so terrible about being a knight of the realm?" As far as I was concerned, let the King sign my scholarship and let me carry on doing what I was already doing. It was all very natural to me and it didn't even occur to me to chase another dream."

"Ah, fair enough," She said, nodding.

"Do you like The Festival of Scholars? He enquired.

"Do I?" Hell, yeah! She said punching the air.

"It's part of our culture, as much as trading is." She exclaimed excitedly.

"What's your favourite part?" Ali asked.

"Well, there are so many!" "The Joust, Shinty, Hammer throw, Stoolball, Gameball, Colf, Skittles, Bowls, and Horseshoes," She said, enthusiastically.

"Thanks for the history lesson, Valentina, I am well aware of the events, hell, I have even taken part in some of them." "Besides, there's a few you've missed out." "There's also, Archery, Falconry, the triathlon, and of course fencing, my speciality."

"Oh, sorry mister high and mighty," She said, placing her hands on her hips.

"Look, I am sorry," he said, holding his hands up in surrender. "One thing still remains; which event do you like the most?"

"Well, they are all good, but I like the things that surround the festival. The maypole, the dancers, the toffee apples, the hobby horse racing, but my favourite are the musicians."

"Gia..."

"Gianni is a dream," Ali said, interrupting her.

"Yes!" "How did you know?" She said, sounding surprised.

"Every girl in Tarnuz loves him." Hector's band is better. They used to be in the same band. Now they are frenemies."

"Yes I heard that." "What happened there?"

Ali shrugged. "Artistic differences I guess. You know what musicians are like."

"Yes I think that's what I heard too," She replied, sadly.

Sensing her mood, Ali asked "I think you have just realised we will miss the festival whilst we're away, haven't you?"

"Yes. I have been to every single one." "It will seem strange not to be there."

"There's always the winter one and that is followed very quickly by the spring festival."

"The spring festival is a good warm up to the Scholars, but it's not quite the same."

"That's true, but is also good to see what your predicted grades are going to be. They should retitle the Spring celebrations as "The festival of the mock exam, or the mocks!" He said, enthusiastically.

"It doesn't roll off the tongue though, does it? She said, truthfully.

"No you're right."

"The Scholars do create their own hype and when spring first appears; you can catch musicians practicing and athletes training." She said, snivelling.

"It's okay; I'll miss them too,"

He said and then he cuddled her. He gave her his hanky and when she was calm again he wiped the tears from his own eyes.

We could die on this mission and the previous year's scholars could have been our last. He thought grimly.

"How did you feel when you graduated?" Ali enquired.

"You're asking me something that happened nearly two years ago!" "I felt special. The festival felt like it was put on just for me, but of course we were celebrating the achievements of all the scholarship graduates." "The festival makes everyone feel special and that's what makes it so charming."

"I can't argue there," Ali said.

We will probably see some peculiar things on this mission." Ali said, changing the subject.

"When you say peculiar, what do you mean? Do you have any examples?" Tina answered.

"Your dad is an old sea dog. He must have told you stories about sea monsters and magnificent beasts."

"My dad used to tell them to me at bedtime and sometimes I would wake up terrified!" she said, as the ship lurched and she fell forward, brushing his hat off his head. She picked it up and handed it to him. It was a cross between a fez and a gold turban.

"Are you a Sheik?"

"No," He said, dusting it off, and putting it on, covering his dark brown centre parting. "It belonged to my father."

"So, we were talking about strange creatures. Have you seen any?" She said.

"That's a tough question to answer. When you are a child, the entire world is exciting, so a flea-ridden dog is an odd animal. There's nothing nice about Sorapis (Serpent) either, unless you are a Sorapis charmer."

"What is it about those guys and the weird flute they use on the horrible reptiles?" She said, miming playing an instrument.

"There isn't any magic in the music they play, I think they hypnotise the beasts by moving the flute."

"Now that makes sense. What makes little sense is why capture a dangerous animal like that?"

"There are two answers to that. Number one: They need to make money just like anyone else and number two: people are fascinated by danger; some are always trying to push boundaries," He said, and then disappeared up the ladder. She stood for a moment and found him drinking water from a flagon.

"Do you think all four of us get motivated by danger?"

"Maybe in part, and also because we are on a royal appointment. The king mentioned something you found. Was it easy to find?" Ali replied

"I wouldn't say easy, no. We had Midnight Spiders to deal with!"

Alessandro shuddered.

"I fell into a pit with a bunch of them once. Scared me half to death! Fortunately, they were babies, and I escaped. I lived terrified for weeks! I was only six!"

"I am not surprised, but what doesn't kill you gives you strength. I think we know that there are monsters out there, it's how we handle it that's the important thing."

He nodded. "I just hope we don't go to war with Khalid."

"Do you always show off in front of royalty?"

He tensed before he answered.

"My dad was highly respected. They were best friends. Daddy was a mighty man of valour and when news of his passing reached the monarch's ear, he tore his robes, put sackcloth on and mourned for a month. He wouldn't eat, and people feared for his health. They allowed father to speak freely, and I thought I had the same privilege, but it turns out I haven't earned it yet."

"That maybe why the king didn't have you executed. You were in serious contempt of the imperial court. What was it you were accusing Nadal of?"

He paused, and then he told her what he saw.

"That is very serious." She said.

"I hope I am wrong, but I think Nadal will try everything within his power to make things difficult for us. He is a powerful man, and I have seen him muttering to himself and mixing bizarre potions late at night in his laboratory."

Valentina shuddered this time. I really hope he is wrong about the Vizier. He sounds very dangerous!

Alessandro crept behind Cilistinu. He was using an Astrolabe. An instrument that could tell time and the position of the sun and the stars. It was a round disc that hung from a pole, and Cilistinu was adjusting it.

"What's the time, Mr Wolf?" Alessandro said.

"One O'clock," he said, whirling around with gritted teeth and fingers curled.

"Ooo, scary," He said, mocking him.

"Ah, lighten up, Ali. It's fun!"

"I am aware of the serious nature of this assignment. I don't want to go to war, and I am worried that if we fail, that's what will happen."

Stinu slumped next to him. "You can't get upset about what hasn't happened, may never happen. It makes sense that you feel this way. You have lost so much already, I know how you feel. I lost my beloved Diana when she was giving birth to Valentina. I still miss her, but I always carry her here," He said placing his fist over his heart.

"You don't understand," Ali said, and disappeared below deck. Stinu said nothing and carried on adjusting the disc.

The smell and sound of frying onions floated towards him and he felt hungry. His mother preparing lunch always satisfied, unless it was a failed experiment. They ended up in the bin or the cat, but that rarely happened.

"What are you cooking mum," He said as he hugged her. She hugged him back, and she kissed him on the cheek.

"Oh, this is a surprise. We have bread, ham, cheese and tomatoes for lunch." She pointed at table with the food on it. "Help yourself."

"Aren't I allowed a little sneaky peaky?" He said lifting the tea towel from the sauté pan. She slapped his fingers.

"You know you're not allowed to know until I am satisfied first!" Her brown eyes blazed with fury and she turned her head so quickly, her brown plait jerked.

"Okay, I am out of here!"

"Tell the crew the lunch is ready."

"I will, I will." He disappeared, and a minute later, the crew arrived, noisily chatting and laughing. She smiled to herself. She still got a buzz from preparing and serving food.

Nadal's ship weighed anchored a mile away, and he regarded the comings and goings on the ship through his telescope.

Chapter Three

After three days, they arrived on the island. The ground was divided between lush vegetation and desert. Valentina gave them the history of the place.

"The Dyidians developed a system of reclaiming the dry sandy soil and making it useful."

"How did they do that?" Ali asked.

"They reintroduced plant life, redirecting water and adding nutrients back into the soil. Then they cultivate the land."

"Fascinating, what ingredient are we here for?"

"We are here for olive oil," Vernu said, pushing past them like an excited child.

"Okay, let's go!" Stinu said.

They made their way through figs, plums, peaches, nectarines, Wisanels (Morello Cherries) and last of all, olives. They gathered the olives into their baskets and feasted on Wisanels, the dark juices running down their chins. Close to them, camels grazed.

Nadal's ship The Tempester was hidden behind a large rock formation. His telescope marked out its prey, and he rummaged around in a sack. He pulled out four Sorapis and dropped them on the floor. He poured a purple powder on the animals and muttered some strange words. The serpents slithered towards the gang and they grew and grew until each one was seven metres long! The explorers carried on filling their baskets.

"Is that a hissing sound, or am I hearing things?" Alessandro said.

"I can't hear anything," Valentina said with a mouthful. Her father scowled at her.

"Wait, I heard something." the captain said,

They turned and saw enormous snakes coming their way with hunger in their eyes!

"Run!" The Admiral shouted, and they rushed towards the camels. They mounted them and the humped creatures took off at a good pace. One reptile nipped at the heel of Ali's animal, but with of a flick of the reigns, he sped up, leaving the pursuers behind. They dismounted and ran up the gangplank. They watched as the Bedouins fought off their attackers. Some screamed in terror and the heroes looked away as the ship glided towards its destination. Nadal collapsed his telescope, kicked the sand and marched back to his vessel.

Chapter Four

Ali watched them lunge forward with their Nimchars for the twenty-fourth time. He had worked them very hard, and they panted and sweat dripped from their foreheads.

"Let's do it again!" he said. The crew groaned.

"You are pushing us too hard!" Tina said, breathless.

"Okay last time." He said pacing up and down with folded arms. "Okay, you can relax now." The crew dropped their swords, muttering to themselves.

Stinu beckoned him over.

"You will get more respect if you treat the crew better, you know."

"I knew this would happen. Nobody is trained to the same standards as me."

"They will improve and we will be armed next time," Stinu said, *he* held up his sword and swiped it through the air. The sun caught the tip of the blade and it shone.

"I don't want anyone to get hurt," he said, walking away. Stinu watched him leave and carried on practicing on the fencing dummy.

Vernu pushed her plate away as if she was trying to hide something. She was.

"What are you up to, mother?"

Her chewing movements were over the top, and she rolled her hands forward. Then she swallowed.

"Nothing that concerns you!"

"Okay, answer this: Are you happy with your results?"

She nodded with excited wide eyes.

"I am thrilled. Run along now!"

She's always like this when she's testing a new dish.

He thought. A short walk to his left and he found Stinu and Tina leaning over a table. Stinu's dark curly head was nodding. They folded the map, and the Admiral started rummaging through his chest. He emerged after two minutes holding a large lump of beeswax, giving Ali two small pieces. Stinu place them in his ears, and Alessandro did the same. The captain handed him a piece of paper. Alessandro unfolded it "Nixas." It read and his heart sped up.

Nixas appear at first, to be beautiful flying mermaids, with voices of angels, but when they swoop in for an attack, their teeth sharpen and their fingernails become talons. They can use their beauty and their haunting songs to lure sailors to their deaths.

Tina and her father tore off small buds of wax and handed them to the crew. Eyes skyward, the gang could see what looked like birds circling overhead. Every now and again, the sun would catch their glistening silver bodies. A song started up, and Ali pushed the buds further into his ears. As the Nixas drew closer, they saw that people had shielded their ears.

Nixa eyes turned red and their gums filled with fangs. One creature dived and grabbed an unfortunate sailor from the deck and flew higher. She dipped the man in out of the sea and drowned him, she released him, and his body fell, making a large splash. Tina's crossbow bolt ended the beast, and it fell backwards into the ocean with a shriek, creating a wave. A spin of the pilot's wheel and the ship lurched to the left, but Galaxio couldn't shake his attacker. It lifted him into the air with cries for help. He nearly died, but a crossbow bolt saved him. He hurtled back to earth. A gang of men caught him and took him below deck. Ali's arrow hit a Nixa in the eye and it plummeted into the ocean. The remaining three formed an arrow formation and assaulted the crew. The crew stood back to back and hacked at the monsters with their swords. Alessandro felt talons buckle his armour on his shoulder as they carried away him.

Satisfied with the chaos on-board the Sebill, Nadal put away his telescope and smiled to himself. Waves lapped against his ship, and he allowed his gaze to settle on the ocean.

***

Growing up, Nadal worked harder to get noticed. Being the second in line to the throne meant he wouldn't be crowned king.

Never an extrovert, he busied himself exploring the many rooms of the palace. One day, he found a winding staircase with strange smells coming from below. Pink flickers danced off the stone walls. Muttering could be heard, so he tiptoed cautiously down the steps. He entered a medium-sized room and saw a bald man. The man had a band of wiry white hair around his ears, ending at the nape of his neck. The man dripped a droplet of pink liquid onto a toad that sat on the bench in front of him. Suddenly, the toad grew twice its size! Startled by what he perceived, he stumbled backwards and knocked over chemistry equipment. The scientist span round and pushed his half-rimmed glasses further up his nose.

"So, it would appear I have a royal meddler! What brings you here, young prince?" He said waving a crooked finger at Nadal?

"I, err, I am very impressed with what I have just seen!" He meant to say more, but the words tumbled out. The scientist relaxed.

"Impressed, eh?" He said, squinting at the boy's face. "This is your lucky day. I need a new assistant. The previous one had an unfortunate accident," he said, as he moved his thumb over his shoulder, pointing at the toad.

Nadal's colour drained from his face, and he tried to get back up the stairs. The mad professor stamped his foot, fell backwards and wiggled his tiny legs in the air, laughing until tears ran down his rosy cheeks. He got up again.

"The look on your face was priceless. I was just joking. I am professor Marvello. People call me the

Magnificent Marvello, or was it Marvello the Magnificent?" "I forget now. Anyhow, pleased to meet you!" he thrust out a small hand from his white lab coat that looked like it had shrunk in the wash.

"I am prince Nadal."

"Ah, you are Nadal and the other one must be Stefano. What brings you to the bowls of the castle?" He said with a smile like a mischievous pixie.

"I often wander the castle grounds looking for a new adventure. Please, good sir, could you tell me what happened to your assistant?"

The professor scratched his ear, stroked his long goatee beard and said: "Oh nothing. I had taught him everything I knew, and he moved on. I think he is King Khalid's chief physician now."

"Wow, that is amazing! Could you teach me everything you know?"

So, this was day one of four years of weird and wonderful experiments. (The toad returned to its proper size that evening)

Shortly after starting with professor Marvello, Nadal could give magic shows to his friends. Some gasped, and some clapped and cheered. Then, after four and a half years studying, the sweet old man died.

After the funeral, Nadal, overcome with grief, smashed up the laboratory. His hands bled from cutting himself on bottles, he fell to his knees and yelled at the top of his voice. This was the day that he changed. He stopped being a fun loving child who enjoyed finding out new things and turned into a bitter and twisted young man.

Stefano became king, The King offered him the job as vizier and he took the job without argument. It delighted him he could deceive the Monarch, and he was giddy with the power. Nadal used mind control potions to make the king do what he wanted. He tore his gaze away from the ocean and looked at the ship again. He didn't like what he saw.

Chapter Five

The Nixa carried him away. His armour protected him. Vernu fired her catapult, hitting its tail. The creature yelped and Ali fell.

"Be ready with that blanket lads."

"Yes, mam," the sailors said.

The crew caught him in a blanket, and they lowered him to safety. The monster attacked again, and he threw his sword at its neck. With gurgle and a spray of blood, it dropped dead.

"Thanks for saving my skin, mum."

"It is my job to protect my child. One day you will find out."

"Not too soon, though. I have a lot I want to do first," He replied, shrugging off his armour and running his fingers over the claw marks.

"What do you plan to do with the armour, son?"

"I will keep it as a souvenir!" He said marching off.

"He's very brave," Cilistinu said as he stood next to her.

"It's a bit of a front, to be honest. He still misses his father. I do too," she said, following her son down the stairs.

The Admiral looked after them and said: "I feel your pain. I do."

Galaxio's faced dripped sweat, and Tina mopped his brow. The healing paste she had been testing for months, called a salve, would heal his shoulder in a week. She worked hard to bring his temperature down.

"A man visited me in a dream and told me about a sacred book by the Dyidians. He gave me the coordinates." He gave them to her. "Promise me you will go right away?"

Although Tina was a Dyidian nut, she was sceptical.

"I can't jeopardise the entire mission for an old book. What's so special about it, anyway?"

"He told me everything I had done wrong that I needed to repent. It terrified me and I obeyed him. I wept, but he gave me peace. It was the strangest thing."

She looked at him and continued to wipe sweat from his head.

"Do you believe the book is genuine?"

"I think this book could change our lives." She handed the rag to a nurse.

"I'll talk to my father and see what he makes of it."

"Okay, I don't think you will regret it."

A light breeze blew the sails, and the boat creaked and moaned. The moon and sea gave tranquillity. Father and daughter sat looking at the moon.

"I don't know if the fever had upset Galaxio said he dreamt about a book."

Stinu put down his wooden bowl and walked to the back of the ship. He paced between moonbeams, rubbing his black and grey beard. Then he faced her, with wide eyes and hands in the air.

"I had the same dream," he said, nodding. Tina dropped her spoon in her bowl. Dinner wasn't a priority anymore, so they scoffed down their meal, eager to plot a fresh course.

He adjusted his Astrolabe. He plotted an alternative route. After they looked at the map, they marked lines to the new destination. He changed course.

Ali fell out of bed. He got dressed and climbed the stairs, and then he confronted the captain.

"My boy, I must change direction, because of my dream last night!" He said, looking wild.

"Have you lost your mind? This is crazy! We are on an important mission, a matter of life and death. It could mean the difference between war and peace."

"Galaxio and I had the same dream. There has to be something in it!"

"Listen to yourself! Do you know how far-fetched this sounds?" It was the last thing he said.

***

An aching head and a sweaty bed woke him. A sultry breeze blew as he got up.

Rubbing the side of his neck, he could feel a spot there. Vernu gave him a bowl of lamb stew and crusty bread. He dipped his bread in the bowl and ate ferociously.

"Steady on, son. You'll give yourself hiccups!"

"Sorry, mum. I am famished."

"I am not surprised. You have been asleep for three days! I found this sticking out of your neck." She handed him a dart with a red feather. "Who did this?"

"Have a guess."

"Do you think it was Tina?"

"Yes I do," He said, placing the empty bowl on his bedroom cabinet. He got up and found Tina. And thrust the dart in her face.

"What's this all about?" He retorted.

She looked at him guiltily. She traced a circle with her foot on the deck, hands behind her back.

"We had to take a chance. Two men had the same dream! We should investigate,"

He looked impressed, but tried not to show it.

"Can't we look into after the principal mission?" "You didn't have to drug me!" He yelled, and breathed heavily, balling his hand into a fist.

"It worried me you would object."

"I can't object when I am asleep."

"That's my point; anyway, we're here now."

"I guess you leave me no choice but to help you."

"You always have a choice. It would be easy for you to stay on The Sibell and polish your armour, or something." 'We could always ask someone else," Tina said, feigning courage. His anger terrified her.

"Fine, I'll help you." He fetched his mum, and they grabbed weapons and exploring equipment and lowered a rowing boat to the sea.

***

From the shore, exotic birds sang to them. And somewhere, a monkey howled. Streams flowed and palm trees dropped coconuts and pineapples. They moved deeper in the everglade and they heard crickets. They came to an ancient graveyard. Broken granite tomb stones littered the ground. A crow squawked from a head stone and flew past them. A stone slid open and a five bony fingers slide the slab to the ground. Bones clacked together, and an armed skeleton emerged from its eternal rest.

He held a sword in one hand and a shield in the other. There was more clacking, and the heroes faced seven more, also armed. The leader stroked his sword on his shield, and the others copied. With bony hand in the air, the leader threw a metal ball on the ground. On impact, it exploded and dust separated the adventurers. Composed entirely of bone, they were surprisingly agile. The skeletons circled, and then attacked. Alessandro jumped back as the leader lunged with an overhead blow. Like a charging bull, the leader's attack was relentless. After fighting, grunting and dodging, Ali's energy was spent. A bony foot kicked him to the ground.

Chapter Six

After along and dusty journey, gruff voice
arrived at Agune Grenze, valley of precious
metals. He dismounted from his camel, took off
his at hat and wiped his forehead with his
kerchief from his shirt pocket. He was grateful
for the loose shirt and baggy trousers. A boy no
more than eleven dropped a basket spilling rocks
on to the dusty floor. The slave master beat him
with a stick and yelled at him in a language he
didn't understand. The rulers came together and
condemned to mining people who had been
found guilty of crimes or prisoners of war.
People who were falsely accused were thrown
into prison. Sometimes, their relatives worked
with them too. They were bound with chains,
working unceasingly by and day through the
night. They had no respite from their captors.
They were carefully cut off from any means of
escape. The language barrier prevented a rapport
from being established between prisoner and
guard, stopping friendship and soft guardians led
to mistakes. More boys entered tunnels made by
galleries formed by the removal of rock,
laboriously gather up the rock as it is cast aside

piece by piece and carry it to the entrance. Older workers over the age of thirty take this quarried stone from them and with iron pestles.

Clepta, you are here to do a job. Not liberate a slave population. Gruff voice thought to himself. He wiped his head again and watched a tall, slim brown skinned, man with a pencil moustache, walked towards him. The man smiled a cruel smile and offered his hand and Clepta shook it.

"Nice to see you again old friend," the thin man said, in a smooth voice that could be used to sweet talk you into a deal or stab you with a concealed small dagger.

"Nice to see you too, Kati," Clepta said, after letting go of the firm handshake.

"What can I do for you today?" Kati said. They passed skilled workers, who rubbed powder on inclined marble boards, pouring water over it as they worked, washing the dirt away. This separated the precious metal from the soil. It was then placed in vessels with equal amounts of lead and barley and covered with a tight fitting lid, which was smeared with mud.

"That batch will be baked for five days before it is ready. Will you be staying long enough for this batch to be ready? I can have your room prepared," Kati said.

"I wanted to ask you about deceiving people," Clepta said, wringing the brim of his hat.

Kati smiled his cruel grin.

"You need to speak to my brother; Abdul. He is very skilled in this matter and will have exactly what you need."

"Very good," Clepta swallowed and then he cleared his throat.

"Could you introduce me please?"

"Of course. Abdul, I have some here who wants to meet you."

A tall man stood up he also had a thin moustache. He was Kati's twin. He shook Clepta's hand.

"What do you have in mind?"

"A very professional job."

"That is my speciality. Happy to help."

"Good, very good." Clepta said, feeling like a mouse being sized up by two Sorapis.

<u>Chapter Seven</u>

Ali gripped his Nimchar but it felt like a lead sledgehammer in his hands. Gripping his sword with both hands, he swiped at his enemy's calf and it snapped and his foe collapsed in a heap like a broken xylophone. Then he laid his head in the sand allowing him to regain his breath.

Vernu beheaded another. Tina cut off a monster's legs. Stinu finished his with a chest blow. They finished the remaining enemies, and then moved on.

A two-hour mountain climb brought them to a cave. After lighting their torches, they descended a sandy bank. They heard the sounds of a stream and scurrying feet. They came to a rock ledge just above their heads. Cilistinu squatted with his back to the ledge and interweaved his fingers. Alessandro stood on his palms and Cilistinu vaulted the fifteen-year-old to the level above. Valentina was next, then Vernu and last of all, the captain. As they rounded the narrow pathway, they faced a three metre long rat. The rodent's eyes glowed red; it opened its mouth and charged them. And they jumped down. Alessandro stabbed its belly drawing blood and Valentina poked her sword in its ear. It spun wildly and knocked Cilistinu out. Vernu fired a flaming arrow, and the vermin fell down the ravine in a fiery display. Vernu opened a vial and waved it under Stinu's nose. As he sat up, he blinked. He held the bottle and said:

"What did you give me? It smelt like dead fish!"

"It's a smelling liquid to wake people. I make it from dead fish!" She said, helping him to his feet.

"Well, it woke me up. Let's hope we don't see any more giant rats!"

"Agreed, lets grab the book and get out of here!" Alessandro said.

Vernu saw Valentina admiring the smelling liquid.

"I'll give you the recipe, if you promise not to dart my son again."

"I promise I won't do that again."

"Okay, but I am not happy with your underhanded tactics."

"There will be no more secrets."

"I appreciate that, but you need to earn my trust. It's difficult to forgive you." She grabbed Tina's hand and squeezed the dart into it. Then she pushed passed her. Ali looked at her as they passed and mouthed "Sorry."

"Hell has no fury like a woman's scorn," Stinu said to his daughter.

"I have been such a fool. We have faced death and we need to count on each other."

"Well, let's hope you have learnt your lesson." Stinu replied.

"You were up for this too!"

"You also need to learn a lesson!"

"Point taken, I think we need to show each other more respect."

The path led to church ruins. As Stinu pushed the door, the wood splintered. Sunlight streamed through a hole in the roof. Vines over hung the rafters. Branches pierced stained glass windows. Broken pews littered the floor. And on the altar sat an old book. The floor had sixteen stone slabs. Six red stones formed vertical lines. Behind the altar, there were stone doors.

Tina threw a stone onto the slabs, and nothing happened. Her father stepped onto a plate. Spears shot out of the opposite wall and Stinu jumped backwards before they impaled him.

"Dad, Vernu, stay here. I want to try something," Valentina said, stepping onto the stones. This time, nothing happened. Alessandro stepped onto the stones. And he was fine. Valentina picked up a block and placed it at the top of the centre line. Alessandro did the same. They used the remaining two blocks to place at the bottom, forming an "I" shape. The ground shook and dust fell on them. But there were no spears this time.

"Why don't you try making an arrow shape?" Vernu suggested.

"You might have a point," Valentina said.

"What's the worst that could happen? We could all end up as kebabs," Ali said sarcastically.

They tried the arrow formation, and the stones rumbled and the teenagers ran back to their parents. The stones parted, revealing orange sand underneath, and the stone doors opened. Ali snatched the book, and they ran through the doors. As they ran, the doors closed, and the temple shook. They ran down the mountainside, passing greenery. As they ran, the temple collapsed. They ran back to their boat and rowed back to the ship.

__Chapter Eight__

Lighting a lantern, Valentina examined the ancient book. She loathed Dyidian lessons at school, but she learnt to love them and she smiled to herself. The book was easy to read, and she absorbed its wisdom with wide-eyed wonder. She translated it in to Raetic.

Ali read up about the next island and its wildlife. After he finished, he laid on his bed swishing his sword in the air. He got up and practiced on the fencing dummy. Whilst he practiced, he felt the cold steel of a blade at the nape of his neck. He turned and saw Stinu holding his Nimchar in front of his own face.

"Do you fancy a duel, good sir?" The older man said.

Ali smiled a sly grin.

"Sure, I'll kick your butt, old man." "A duel to first blood?"

"Of course, Ali, let's be gentleman about it."

"Absolutely," Ali said, raising his sword.

They crossed swords, and the fight begun. Their swords clanged and clashed, and Stinu pulled the younger man's sword to the deck. He kicked Stinu's shin, and he lunged forward, pointing his

50

sword at the other man's neck. Stinu flicked his sword away, and it imbedded itself in the decking, wobbling. He retrieved his weapon and Stinu tried to slash Ali's left shoulder, but Ali blocked the blow. Swords locked and Stinu used his body weight to push against Ali, but Ali broke free. Stinu lunged and came in close, but Ali's foot shot out and kicked him in the stomach winding him.

"Have you had enough yet?" Ali said, taunting him.

"No. first blood, remember," Stinu said, in between pants.

"Very well, Ali said, and helped the Admiral to his feet. Feet planted, they faced each other again. With bent knees and Nimcha at shoulder level, Ali went in for an overhead strike, but Stinu side stepped and followed with a cut to Ali's right side, but Ali's jumped to his left, and then he grabbed a rope and swung towards Stinu, kicking his sword out of his hand. Dropping to the ground, he ran over to the man and kicked him in the stomach, a foot placed on his chest; he pointed the tip of the blade at his Adam's apple, and then swiped Stinu's cheek drawing first blood. Stinu surrendered and Ali helped him up.

The young man whirled his sword around and sheathed it.

"I will fight you again."

"You got lucky, Ali. I was letting you win."

"Yeah, yeah, whatever. I won fair and square and you know it."

"We shall see. I think we both enjoyed ourselves!"

"Yes, I think we did."

Later that night, someone slid a piece of parchment under Ali's door. He took it back to bed and looked at it.

It read "I know the plans I have for you says The Lord. They are good plans. To give you a future and a hope." Jeremiah 29:11.

"Wow," he said, as the hairs on his arms stood up.

"We might have a chance at success. I need to think about this message." Ali said, trying to take in the meaning of the words.

The detour made them arrive late on the "Island of rice." Ali briefed them on its inhabitants and the best form of defence. He agreed with the crew they would send a crow for reinforcements or a dove for peace. They moored their rowing boat and took cautious steps through the paddy fields. They could see a hunched backed old lady, but he warned them not to underestimate her. She attacked them with deadly acid venom, but their armour protected them against her.

Then they slashed her back. She yelled and span round. She flung her venom at Vernu, but Vernu sidestepped. Vernu lunged at her opponent, but the hag side stepped. The hag opened her mouth and sprayed acid at Vernu. Some of it caught her should armour and the shock made her yell. Distorting her face, she shouted and charged plunging her sword into the monster's heart. The hags head jerked violently and the heroes scattered as more venom sprayed the area. They watched the hag die and Vernu retrieved her sword and then they opened a dove cage and sent a bird back to the ship, and the crew helped them harvest the rice. They left a detachment of men to farm the fields, and then they sailed on.

Their next ingredient was chicken. They had chicken in Tarnuz, but Khalid had rationed food until they returned. Ali saw him as a bully, but he didn't want to get his throat cut for disobedience.

Back on the boat, Tina checked Galaxio's wound. It had healed well.

"Thank you for believing me, about the book mistress."

"Don't mention it. Two men with the same dream? Amazing!"

Galaxio looked disappointed.

"Forgive me. I didn't mean to dismiss you. If it makes you feel any better, if my dad had been ill, I wouldn't have believed him, either!"

He turned on his side.

"The wisdom in that book is life changing, I am certain!" He said sounding positive, but didn't feel it.

Tina changed the subject.

"Your wound is healing very well. I'll check you again tomorrow," She said, turning to leave. He stopped her.

"When you have translated more of the book, please let me have a copy?"

"I will do that. I don't think the book is complete. It feels like there are bits missing, but I will give you what I have," She said truthfully, tapping his good shoulder.

He nodded, and his curly blonde hair shook. His blue eyes were helpless and innocent. She felt bad for doubting him. She took the stairs to the deck. Ali peered through a telescope. He put it down when she stood next to him.

"I read your parchment, interesting, very interesting."

"I know the plans I have for you," says the Lord. "They are plans for good, to give you a future and a hope." Jeremiah 29:11. "Is that the one?"

"Yes, that's it. It made me think. He turned and looked at her. I think we are going to succeed."

"You had a lack of faith about our quest?"

"Yes. We have already encountered dangerous characters and anyone of them could have meant death for all of us. Those skeletons at the graveyard gave me the creeps," he said, shuddering.

"I always thought you were this tough warrior type, a leader of men."

"Having feelings doesn't make you weak. You can read about an enemy, study how it moves, how it fights, what weapons it uses, but it's all head knowledge. When you're in the heat of a battle, anything can happen."

She nodded and interlocked her fingers and placed her forearms on the bow of the ship.

"I have checked on Galaxio."

"Oh, how's he doing?"

"He's going to be just fine. It's not complete, you know."

"What isn't complete?" he asked.

"The book we found. I can't help thinking we have found only part of it,"

"What makes you think that?"

"Well, it refers to past events, but those bits are missing."

He leant back and looked at her.

"I have questions about the guy in the dream." 'Who is "The Lord?"

"I wondered that myself, maybe he owns the book?"

"I guess we will have to wait and see," she said, as the sun set.

Chapter Nine

Four days' sailing, brought them to their destination. They took a rowing boat to the shore.

"We're here!" Stinu announced, more enthusiastically than he needed to. They disembarked, and they saw a courtyard with broken slabs. It had various statues. Some pointed out to sea, whilst others pointed to the island. Some fought each other.

The brown statues were a mixture of men, women and beasts. One statue was a Minotaur. It held a large club.

"Something feels off. I don't like this at all," Vernu said, speaking for everyone.

"It's just a bunch of statues. They can't hurt you," Stinu said, trying to dismiss the idea. Following a stream, they travelled deeper into the island. In the distance, they heard a roaring waterfall. A large blue butterfly, with a wingspan the size of a dinner plate landed on an exotic flower, moved its wings and then it flew off. Ali pointed at a multi-coloured bird in a tree.

"Look, up there!" He said, and the adventurers watched it fly away.

"This is paradise!" Tina said.

As they ventured further, Nadal watched from a safe distance. He stood in front of the Minotaur statue and blew a red powder into its nostrils. The brown coating cracked. The face ripped in two revealing skin and horns. Within seconds, the statue had come to life, waiting for instructions.

"Get them!" Nadal said and pointed toward the explorers. With a deep throated bellow and steam coming out of its nostrils, it thundered after them, making the ground shake with heavy footsteps.

"I don't like the sound of that," Ali said.

They turned and saw the Minotaur running towards them. They drew their swords and prepared for the fight. Without warning, the fiend aimed its club at Cilistinu, but he dodged and it hit a tree, splitting it in half, sending pink blossom flying. The flowers landed on Ali and Tina. They liked a bride and groom! Tina climbed on the tree and then she leapt on to the rocky ledge on her left. Wasting no time, Ali slashed at the demon cutting its thigh. It roared in pain and banged its club on the ground knocking Ali off his feet. Vernu fired an arrow into its shoulder. After roaring, the Minotaur's club crashed down next to Vernu, also rendering her unconscious. Stinu leapt from a nearby tree and aimed at the creature's neck, but missed. The Minotaur grabbed Stinu by the face and threw him to the ground like a discarded toy. He groaned and rolled over. Seeing her fallen father, blind fury consumed Valentina.

"No!" She yelled.

Seeing her on the rock face, the Minotaur started climbing after her. In terror, she rang further up the mountain. Finding a man sized opening, she squeezed herself in and hid behind a rock formation. Summoning her courage, she peered around the rocks and saw the eye of the Minotaur darting about trying to find its prey. Without thinking, she resumed her hiding place; her breaths were frightened gasps as she tried to contain her fear. Outside, she heard the Minotaur breathing. Slowly, he moved away.

I have to lure him into a trap.

After deciding to leave her hiding place, she saw hope. Opposite the path was ravine and on the other side of that the mountains continued. She sprinted and then jumped across the chasm, with limbs flailing briefly; her fingers caught the ledge on the other side. Feet scraping at the cliff face, she pulled herself up. Now all she needed to do was get the Minotaur's attention. And then she put her fingers in her mouth and blew.

"Hey, grass breath, over here! She shouted, and waved her hands.

The creature turned around and started running towards her. After she stepped back, he had room to grab the ledge. When his fingers touched the ledge, she drove her sword into the top of his right hand. He yelled in a pain letting go and plummeted to his death. A gasp left her lips as she peered over the edge of the mountain, seeing the twisted corpse of the Minotaur. Carefully, she rested with her back against the rocks. After this, she climbed down the mountain and tended to her fallen comrades. She made them follow her finger with her eyes. She performed other tests for concussion, and after she was satisfied, she helped them to their feet. No one was seriously hurt and she was pleased.

Nadal appeared from hiding and shook his fist at their backs.

"I would hope nobody else tries to kill us today," Vernu said.

"I think they will think twice if they see your skills. You're pretty handy with a long bow," Stinu said to her.

"My husband taught me the basics and then I ended better than him."

"He must have been an excellent teacher."

"The best," she said, staring at her feet, and then she strode ahead.

The roar of the waterfall meant they had to shout.

Freshwater crabs scuttled along the river bank. Vernu killed one with her bow, and then she made a fishing rod from a sapling. She dangled the crab over the water and more crabs gripped on. She hauled her catch ashore and clubbed the crabs. Whilst Vernu caught the crustaceans, Stinu erected tents and Tina and Ali made a fire. The heroes dined on crab meat and slept in their tents.

***

They picked a path behind the waterfall. Narrow pathways made them press against the slippery walls. Carefully, they reached the ledge above. Cautiously they walked on the stepping stones.

The glade beckoned to them. As they followed the river, they had to cross the other side, but crocodiles blocked their path. Alessandro pulled his Sorapis flute out of his bag and played a tune. The music mesmerised the crocodiles and they lined up, providing a deadly walkway. When the tune ended, the reptiles resumed writhing and swimming, preventing their escape.

"Just as I thought. How good are you at music, Valentina?"

"It seems easy enough."

"Right answer!" "I will teach you a simple tune." 'We need to get them to line up again so I can reach those vines.'

True to form, she played the tune and the toothy demons lined up. With feet as light as a summer's breeze, he sprinted across the animal's backs to safety. With great effort, his Jambiya cut through the creepers.

"Here, mum, catch this," He said, flinging a vine across the river. She caught it and swung across as Valentina's flute soothed the grinning monsters.

"Valentina, you will be last. I need you to keep them calm." Vernu flung the plant and Stinu caught it and swung to safety.

"Listen to me. Keep playing until you catch the vine. You'll have about twenty seconds to cross before they realise what happened."

She did as he said, and the beasts got restless. One snapped at her dress as she flew past. Her tiara fell in to the waiting jaws of one fiend, but they escaped.

They climbed a slope and faced a cave-mouth. A stone blocked the entrance. In the centre of the stone, they saw an incomplete picture. They saw a man with a headdress riding a horse. The other tiles lay scattered on the floor.

"Ah, a puzzle!" Valentina said, excitedly.

"Let's try this one," Cilistinu said, placing the man's torso under his neck. The tiles locked into place. "I am so glad I got one right," he said, standing back to admire his handy work.

Vernu placed the horse's rear beneath Cilistinu's tile. And this locked. They cheered.

Alessandro placed the horse's back legs on Vernu's tile and that fitted.

Valentina finished the neck and belly of the horse.

Alessandro's completed the horse's back legs.

Stinu placed the middle tile. There was a click, and the rock rolled away, revealing a downward staircase. With lit torches, they proceeded onwards. The stairs snaked left and right, and they emerged in farmland. Chickens pecked at the ground. They were in the right place. They saw a tall man with messy grey hair feeding the hens.

"I am Entusiatia. There is an easier route on the other side of the island." He said peering at them, showing the whites of his eyes.

"What makes you say that?" Cilistinu said.

"You wouldn't face the crocodiles or the annoying puzzle."

"What would be different if we chose your route?"

"Oh, about two hundred angry natives armed with spears, and the Harpies, of course."

"That's easier?" Alessandro said.

"Oh, yes, much easier. They don't bother me at all."

"How long have you lived here?" The youth said, trying to keep his cool.

"Oh, not long. Twenty years."

"I give up," Alessandro said, walking back to Tina.

"How much do you want for twenty hens, assuming you will carry a cage for us?" Cilistinu asked.

"Two hundred Staters should cover it."

"Two hundred Staters?! I hope these chickens lay golden eggs!" Ali said, rushing forward.

Cilistinu apologised and took Ali aside.

"We aren't spending our own money. It belongs to the king. I know it's a lot, but the alternative is death and destruction. And I don't know about you, but I enjoy living in a peaceful and *complete* Tarnuz," He hissed.

"I guess," He said, looking at the ground.

"Right, let's pay him and go home," He said, and then faced Entusiatia. "We accept your reasonable offer."

"Very good," He said, clapping and bouncing on the balls of his feet. "I will also carry a cage of hens for you." He beckoned, and Stinu handed him a money pouch. He untied the drawstrings and took out a coin and examined it. It had an etching of a lion on its surface, its roaring face immortalised. The lion had a wart on its head, and it flashed in the sunlight. Entusiatia turned it over, inspecting the paw print on the back, and then he swallowed it. It shocked them.

"This is the real coin. It will come out of me."

After an hour, they had five cages, each containing four birds. They made their way to their boat. As they walked down the hill, Harpies descended upon them. They placed the cages on the floor and prepared to fight.

Chapter Ten

"I don't understand. They would never attack me," Entusiatia said, confused.

"It might have something to do with you having guests," Stinu volunteered.

Swords flew, and they slew three harpies. Four more attacked, and they took care of them. Five to go. Vernu felled one with her bow, Ali sliced off a wing of another and it crashed on the beach. Sword drawn, Stinu advanced, but the flying fiend slashed his torso. He cried out and plunged his weapon into the animal's chest, and then he retrieved his sword. Tina fired a silver ball from her catapult straight into the open mouth of a harpy and it swallowed it. With a look of surprise, it exploded and feathers rained down on them. The last harpy grabbed the farmer's cage, but he snatched it back. Ali thrust his sword into the creature's back and it fell.

They made it to the beach, and they heard shouting and running feet. A spear flew, landing in the sand. Without wasting more time, they fled to their boat and rowed away. They made it to their vessel and watched the natives yelling, raising their spears and shields. Entusiatia waved from the shoreline.

Shortly after the ordeal, Tina dressed her father's wounds, but he insisted on piloting the ship. And then Cilistinu collapsed, lying next to the pilot's wheel.

"I will take over." Galaxio said,

"Are you strong enough?" Valentina said.

"I am."

Tina and the others rushed to Stinu's side. They carried him below deck. Sweat poured from his forehead and his torso looked inflamed. Tina took a rag from a bucket of water and wiped his brow. After this, she handed the rag to the nurse, and then looked for the anti-venom. Once she found it, she put it to her father's lips.

"Thank you," he said, returning his head to the pillow. She redressed his cut and withdrew to talk to the others.

"He should be fine within a week. Damn it, we shouldn't have detoured," She said, feeling guilty.

"We did the right thing," Vernu said, placing a reassuring hand on her shoulder.

"I read about that island before landing. They could have attacked us at any moment," Alessandro said, trying to sound comforting.

"Yes, I know, and I am sure he will recover, but he will have strange dreams." Alessandro and Vernu looked at each other.

"What makes you say that," Vernu said, stroking her hair.

"Harpies secrete hallucinogenic venom from their talons," Ali said. "Causing nightmares and visions."

"His screams and night terrors could give us sleepless nights," Tina said

"We can take turns to watch him in the night, can't we, Ali?"

Alessandro glared at her, and she elbowed him in the ribs.

"Oh, right, of course," he said, rubbing his side.

"And all the other times we can use bee's wax, to block out the sounds," She said smiling. Valentina smiled too.

"I would like that. We are a team now. We should look after one another."

"We are all in this together. We will take care of him."

"I think I while train for a while," Ali said, taking the stairs. Shortly afterwards, they heard his Nimchar striking the fencing dummy.

"Is he still blaming himself for the death of his father?"

Vernu nodded.

"We both blame ourselves, but we knew the risky life his father led. It's hard for him. His father was amazing, and he doesn't want to let him down."

"I think Ali is pretty incredible."

"You should tell him that, but he might bite your head off!"

They smiled, and Vernu and Valentina hugged. Tears rolled down Valentina's cheek.

"I know it sounds silly, but I don't want dad to die and I don't want to go to war," She sobbed.

"The Lord will comfort those who mourn in Zion," Vernu said.

Valentina pulled away.

"You have been reading the ancient book too!"

She nodded.

"I am impressed with the truth of the book. It's more than just poetry, although poems are beautiful. Every time I read it, I am encouraged and inspired, able to believe in myself, and I have a sense that we are not alone. Someone is looking over us, someone who cares."

"All I thought was: where is Zion?" Tina said.

They both laughed.

"That is the explorer in you." Vernu said.

"I will sit out the next adventure, if you don't mind. My priority is my father."

"Of course, I'll help Ali pick new men."

"Galaxio is fit enough now. He knows what I know about puzzles. Try to convince him, but I don't think it will take much to persuade him. I kind of get the impression he has found a new confidence. I think it might have come from reading the book."

"That's great; I think we could do with someone who has experience."

Valentina nodded. "If you want experience, he fits the bill."

"All we need is a brilliant navigator and a warrior; one person who will fit into both roles. Your father is a tough act to follow!"

"You're not wrong. I have great faith that dad will be fit next week."

"Have you treated people for Harpy attacks in the past, then?"

"Yes, I have. They were fine afterwards. I wasn't sorry to blow one up!"

"You have a new secret weapon. Please tell me about it."

"I can do better than that," She said, taking down a box from its shelf. "Here, my gift to you."

Vernu opened the box, revealing twelve silver golf sized balls.

"They are exploding catapult shots; they should do the trick,"

Vernu pulled back her empty sling. "But I hope I don't need to use them."

"I hope so too, but we know how dangerous the world is."

"Thanks for this, and we'll fill you in when we get back. Who is taking the first watch for Cilistinu tonight?"

Valentina grinned like a croc. "Ali will do it."

"Have you asked him?"

"No, I thought you could."

"Ah, you were doing so well. I thought we were becoming friends," She said mocking her.

"Look, you're his mother. I thought he would listen to you."

"You're right. He will take the first watch," She said relaxing.

Valentina let out a deep sigh. "Good, I am sorry; I didn't mean to presume anything."

"Its fine, he might protest to begin with, but I think he will be happy to help. He respects him."

"Well, that's settled then. Would you take the next shift?"

"Yes, I can do that for you."

"Excellent. Get some sleep now."

"I'll have a lie down and see what happens."

"Okay, I'll take over from you just before dawn. I'm awake anyway." They parted and Vernu heard her quill scratching upon parchment.

Chapter Eleven

Darkness wasn't a problem for Ali. Tina had given him firefly to drink, and he read the book as if it was daylight. A book this fascinating shouldn't be kept secret. Everyone needed to know about it. Valentina had to copy the text for Tarnuz. Was it possible that a machine could write for her, speed things up? He didn't have the answer.

Cilistinu groaned in his sleep, and then he shot bolt upright, eyes wide, but not really awake.

"She came to me, although it wasn't her."

"Who came, Admiral, who came?"

"My wife, but she was a monster. She had a forked tongue like a snake and black eyes, dark as midnight pools."

Valentina warned them this would happen, that night terrors would plague him with a distorted view.

"Did she say anything?"

"She said we must turn back. She said Nadal would capture you, causing you great pain." Ali went as white chalk. Ali pulled out the knockout liquid and placed it under Stinu's nose. Within seconds, the older man was snoring loudly.

But he couldn't sleep now. Had this dream predicted his death? No, that seemed unlikely, but he needed to stop this prophecy of doom. Nobody likes bad news, but he had a sick man to look after. He fell to his knees and prayed.

"Lord of the old book, you give me a future and a hope. If this terrible nightmare is true, please help me overcome it."

It wasn't a miracle, but he had peace, a peace that he couldn't explain. A few minutes passed, and then he looked at Stinu, sleeping serenely. Satisfied, he carried on reading. Two hours later, Vernu relieved him.

"Let me continue watching him."

"You get some rest."

"I would like to carry on reading."

"That's fine, but you get to bed. I've got this."

"Okay, thanks." He settled in his bed, but the manuscript fell to the floor as he drifted off to sleep.

In the morning, he went to the kitchen, and a junior cook prepared breakfast. The chickens had laid more eggs and the whisking sounds made his stomach rumble. Ten minutes later, he tucked into the best scrambled eggs he had tasted in a month. Mother had trained her staff well.

Three days of Cilistinu's intense dreams had left the heroes exhausted, but he had recovered well.

"I am as fit as an ox. I could beat Ali with one hand behind my back!" Cilistinu said

.

Ali stopped twirling the coloured ball between his fingers and puffed his chest against Cilistinu's. Everyone ran up the stairs. Sailors tapped each other on the shoulders; others whispered to each other, some gestured with their thumbs. Some had a wager on him.

Bruno, a muscular sailor with a curly moustache and a goatee beard, tied Stinu's left hand behind his back. People cheered, and they placed bets. The two fighters sized each other up. Thronged by the crowd and spurred on by their cheers and shouts, their swords clanged together announcing the contest. With a tremendous eruption of noise the crowd's excitement gave Cilistinu confidence.

He lunged at Ali, swiping at his throat, but Ali sidestepped and moved the sword out of the way. Swords clashed again in a flurry of speed and steel. Surprised at his speed and strength, Ali had to think quickly. He rolled a beer barrel at his attacker, but Cilistinu jumped over the object and landed deftly on his feet.

The mob roared, and Stinu cracked his neck from left to right, beckoning Ali with his fingers. With teeth clenched and a wild look in his eyes, Ali charged with an overhead attack, but Stinu blocked and jumped backwards.

Ali followed with rapid slashes at Stinu's torso but he dodged. Ali extended his arms making the sword into a long point, but Stinu jumped backwards. Ali let his sword hang forward and down, with the point dipping at a steeper angle, Stinu came close and Ali head-butted him. Stinu shook his head and saw floaters in his eyes. Ali rounded him and waited for his opponent to regain his composure.

Stinu performed a cross strike, but Ali blocked and then he pulled away. Clang, clang, clang went the swords as each man tried to outdo his foe. Out of breath, they circled each other, sizing each other up.

Ten minutes passed, and Stinu disarmed Ali, pinning him with hit and he pointed his sword at his throat.

Like a swarm of bees, the sailors pressed against their champion, one ruffled his hair, and then the Admiral passed out.

When he awoke, Valentina's face was a shimmering blur. As his vision improved, he could see an angry frown creasing her pretty forehead.

"Somebody once said: Men never grow up. You have proved them right," She said, getting up and wringing the rag angrily.

"I won, didn't I? Doesn't that prove I am fit to join you on the next quest?"

"You passed out. That proves to me you still need rest!" She said, looking like a huffing bull.

"Besides, Bruno and Galaxio are replacing both of you," Ali said. "Valentina has agreed to it. Get better, because I want a rematch."

"But I can do this mission." He tried to sit up, but the room spun and he lay down again.

"Take some more time, we've got this," Ali said, massaging his shoulder. Cilistinu rubbed the young man's shoulder.

"Perhaps I was a little too hasty. Bruno is one of my finest men. He is a fine warrior. I'll see you all when you get back."

Ali smiled and left them to it.

Chapter Twelve

After sailing for a day they reached the island known as Zalon, which means "shadow"

Snow and icy winds made their arms ache and the oars felt as heavy as lead, but they pulled the boat to safety and secured it.

Night was two hours old, and it was hard to see. The wind blew snowflakes that stung like small icy daggers. Wolves moved in the distance and one howled, the pack echoed.

With their swords drawn they advanced they formed a tight huddle, making sure they kept the wolf pack in front of them. Vernu lit a torch and stabbed at the leader it. She then started yelling and making herself as tall as she could. The other heroes copied her. Eyes shifted across the landscape, taking in the terrain. Suddenly, a wolf the size of two men, snarled at them, top lip curled dripping with saliva. It had hungry eyes. It leapt grapping Galaxio's arm. Swords cut it down. It yelped and then fell.

Before they knew it, the pack had trapped them. They scaled a ledge and Vernu climbed a tree, and crouched there. She shot a wolf in the eye with her crossbow. Ali killed another wolf. Each adventurer had a lit torch in one hand and a sword in the other. A combination of lunging with swords and torches and lots of shouting yielded an exhausted victory and they finally overcame the pack.

"In here," Galaxio said, finding the entrance to a cave. When they were safely inside, Bruno rolled a stone into place and it secured them. Vernu, being the least injured, bandaged Galaxio's arm and tended the wounds of the others. Four torches enabled them to see, and Ali lit more so that Vernu could cook. They dined on beef stew and dumplings. His mother's cooking always surprised Alessandro.

In the morning, they reheated the stew, and then they rolled the stone away. Fresh snow carpeted the ground, and the air was still and crisp.

Cautiously, they walked through the snow, hoping they wouldn't disturb unsavoury wildlife. As they passed a ledge, they heard a snorting sound. A Humanoid with white fur glanced at them. It was six metres tall. It had large dark eyes and curly white horns on both sides of its head.

Its blood curdling roar made the snowfall from the ledges; it beat its chest and leapt down landing in front of them. More snow fell, and they heard a rumble higher up the mountain. Without hanging around, they ran. The yeti was fast, but they were faster.

Vernu fired her catapult. There was an explosion, and the yeti writhed in agony, but it still kept coming. The others fired flaming arrows at the beast, making it angry. It charged at Ali. At the last minute, he rolled. Unable to stop itself the, monster plummeted to its death.

"You may have escaped the yeti, but you won't escape an avalanche," Nadal said to himself from his lookout higher up the mountain. After prising a large boulder free with his staff, he sent it rolling down the hill after them. Slowly, the rock gained speed, and the adventurers saw it heading towards them.

A quick whistle from Galaxio and Zilli swooped down, and they climbed on his back and they soared away from danger. Zilli had been following their journey from the beginning. Every now and again, Ali thought he saw a large eagle above the ship, but dismissed it. Now he wanted to kiss the bird, but he stroked his neck instead. With an appreciative squawk, the bird flew downwards after it had found safety, he landed and the grateful travellers disembarked. Galaxio thanked their feathered rescuer and took out a dead rabbit from his shoulder bag, and the bird gently took it from him. After a pat on the neck, the bird flew away.

"I think we were in a tight spot," Vernu said, and they nodded.

They flew for a day, and this part of the island was completely different. There were palm trees and running streams. A humming bird passed them and they saw monkeys swinging through the trees. A Sorapis slid into the stream and headed downriver. There were trees ladened with fruit. Some fruit were peaches the size of watermelons. Smaller ones looked like nectarines. There were trees with spiky fruit on them and others contained grapes.

"Okay, so where's the danger?" Ali said sarcastically.

"Danger is all around us. Be on your guard," Bruno said in a thick accent Ali couldn't identify.

"I couldn't agree more. Did you see that Sorapis?" He said, wide eyed.

"I am glad it went the other way, but my sword is sharp," Bruno said, whipping his sword in front of him.

"Save it for combat. I am happy with my ears staying on my head, thank you!"

"Sorry, I am always ready, willing to protect and serve."

"Glad to hear it and it sounds like I can count on you in a crisis."

"That you can young sir that you can."

Smoke came from the riverbank and they smelt fish and cooked fruit. Vernu called them over. They sat on smooth stones around the fire and Vernu handed them all a warm banana skin. Ali unwrapped it and it contained a beautiful red fish cooked with onions and a yellow fruit cut into rings.

After they had eaten, Vernu flicked her head round.

"I thought I heard something," She said.

"Ali, did you hear anything?" He nodded and looked over her shoulder. Giant scorpions the size of elephants moved towards them. Ali jumped, and the others jumped too. One arachnid grabbed Vernu with its pincers, hoisting her into the air. Ali sprung into the air and sliced off the pincer, freeing his mother, and then he drove his sword into the creature's neck. It twitched and then died.

They chased Galaxio in circles around a tree. If you were watching, you would have laughed, but Galaxio was taking it seriously. With the scorpion's tail in front of him, he chopped off the sting. The monster turned to charge, but Galaxio threw his sword at its head, killing it. Ali stood in front of a rock face. A beast scuttled towards him and flicked its tail. With quick thinking and a bit of luck, he dodged, and the sting embedded itself in the rock. A quick leap and Ali landed on its back, and he thrust his sword into the creature's head. Pincers flew and Bruno's sword clanged against them.

Man and beast entered into a grotesque dance. Scuttling forward, the beast nipped at Bruno and each time, the warrior leapt backwards trying to avoid the deadly pincers. The creature flicked its sting at him, and Bruno blocked it. With his sword at his hip, he lunged at the beast's head and wounded it. Angry now, the beast shot forward and landed on his blade, limping, the animal fled, leaving a heavy blood trail behind it. But Bruno lost his footing and slid down stream. Even his great strength couldn't stop him from being buffeted by the rushing rapids. They tried rescuing him with ropes and branches, but he couldn't grab them. It wouldn't be long before the waterfall carried him to his death, if they didn't rescue him soon. One last attempt with Galaxio's lasso and they pulled Bruno to safety. They collapsed on the riverbank, panting.

When they had recovered, they moved on.

Everything seemed peaceful. Warmed by the afternoon sun and soothed by birdsong, they tried to relax. Danger lurked everywhere. A dusty path gently sloped into longer grass. Soon they walked through wheat and they cut some with their swords storing it in their backpacks. Beyond the field lay thick woodland that the sun couldn't penetrate. It was silent in the forest.

"The birds know something we don't. If they aren't singing, it can only mean one of two things. One they have gone to bed, but judging by the position of the sun, it's mid-afternoon, so we can rule that out; or, the birds sensed danger," Ali said.

"I have faced death many times. If I die in this wood, make sure I die with honour," Bruno said, clutching his sword, eyes darting left and right.

Before anyone could speak, a big cat growled and a black panther padded towards them, blocking their exit.

"It may not attack. Panthers are solitary animals and are frightened of humans. Don't make any sudden movements, and let's hope he gets bored and moves away," Galaxio said, trying to sound brave, but convincing no one.

The cat growled again bearing its big teeth and began circling the group. Back to back and swords raised, they moved like a large crab. The animal continued to circle them, growling. A bird fluttered from the bushes and the panther ran after it. They watched the cat disappear. After they breathed a sigh of relief, they moved through the wood. When they reached the end, they came to a wooden bridge which spanned a stream.

"People have lived here before," Vernu said.

"Unless the yeti built it," Galaxio said, finding his sense of humour.

Vernu and Ali laughed, Bruno looked backwards, and forwards as they proceeded. Nobody slipped on the sturdy bridge they all made it to safety. A corkscrew path led them to the top of a hill and another path led down. At the bottom of the hill, they saw trees with red apples dangling from the branches. One tree looked ancient and had no fruit or leaves. Ali saw a face in the middle of the tree. After he rubbed his eyes, he saw it wasn't a man's face, but a deer's skull. It had trees for limbs. With a rip of earth, it uprooted itself and moved towards them. Slowly, it raised its arms and the apple trees sprung into life and came towards them.

"Here, put this on your sword," Galaxio said, passing around a glass bottle with gold liquid in it. "This will make your blows more effective."

Barely having time to oil their swords, it attacked them. A large, thick tree root grew out of the creature's arm and snaked along the ground, coiling itself around Ali. It constricted him like a python. Immediately, Bruno's sword freed him and he fell to the ground wheezing and he spat out salvia. Fire leapt from tree to tree as Vernu's fiery arrows destroyed the apple trees.

They groaned and wailed like mourners at a funeral.

"What is this thing?" Ali said,

"It's called a Leshen, ancient and powerful."

"Yes, I have felt its power first hand," He said, watching the creature his mum and Bruno fighting it. Galaxio and he re-joined the fight, and the Leshen was no more. After they dusted themselves off, they advanced further and they came to a gigantic crater. It was a mile long and they couldn't walk around it. Carefully forming a line, they lowered themselves down the rocky sides. An alien environment made them feel like they were on another planet. Bowl shaped and gravely, the large imprint on the land had an eerie stillness. They made it to the other side, and Galaxio used his grappling hook to latch onto a tree on the edge. Once satisfied it could take his weight, he offered the rope to Vernu. The others took up the slack. Ali, Bruno followed her and last of all Galaxio.

When they reached the top, they saw two Bedouins who beckoned them over. They smiled and pointed at their strange animals. At first glance, they looked like horses, but after closer inspection, they saw horse's legs, two camel humps, large lips, bad teeth and big eye lashes.

"Buy Equomel," One of them said pointing at a group of four, eating hay.

"How much are they?" Galaxio said.

The Bedouin held up four fingers on each hand.

"Eight hundred for all four?"

The man shook his head and pointed at one animal.

"Very well," He sighed, handing over four money pouches. The traders talked rapidly and clapped their hands. They fitted each Equomel with a saddle and led them to their animals. Shortly after mounting, they started their journey across the desert. Equomels were perfect for sandy terrain. They were fast as horses but had the endurance of a camel. Four days trekking, led them to a garden guarded by a portcullis. Above the portcullis, there were squares cut into the brickwork. After looking around, they found large coloured gems that looked like they fitted. Green, light blue, orange and dark blue. Bruno being the tallest placed his stone in the first slot. There was an earthquake and the ground split, leaving him and Galaxio on one side and Ali and Vernu on the other.

"I think that was the wrong slot," Ali shouted. "Try another one, but don't get it wrong this time!"

Galaxio looked at his gem. It was green. He handed it to Bruno, who placed it in the first slot. With a grinding of metal, the portcullis raised half a metre.

"It looks like we are getting somewhere," Vernu shouted.

"I think I know what this puzzle might represent," Galaxio shouted. "What colours do you have?"

"We have a light blue and a dark blue."

"Okay, throw me the light blue one first."

Ali did as he asked and once again, Bruno placed the gem. Success! It moved another half a metre.

"Now place your orange stone again."

"I hope you right, Mr Galaxio," he said, showing concern and with good reason. He placed his stone, and the gate moved again.

"Now give me your dark blue stone." They did so and positioned it next to the others. A second tremor hit, and the gorge re-connected. Then the grate returned to the door frame.

"It turns out I was right. The stones are earth, wind, fire and water!" Galaxio said, feeling proud.

High fiving, they walked into a garden with flowers of orange, red, blue, yellow and purple. Some flowers were multi-coloured. There were large butterflies and sometimes they blended in with the flowers. The air was a strange concoction. It smelt of flowers, but it mingled with the smell of chives and onions. Beyond the flowerbed, they heard a water feature. It was a leaping fish with a jet of water gushing from its mouth. Left of the water feature the onions and chives grew. A statue towered over them. It had six arms. It held a sword in each hand. It was bronze, but it had turned green through exposure to the elements.

Something startled the Equomels and the heroes went to their aid. Whilst they turned their backs, Nadal blew a red powder into the nostrils of the statue.

"Live Urudu, live," He said, stepping aside as it came to life. After he threw a powder down, he disappeared in a cloud of purple smoke.

Satisfied that the animals were grazing again, the group returned to the garden as the Urudu scrapped two swords together. It walked towards them, its head moving from left to right as if it was dancing to its own rhythm. With a swing of his grappling hook, Galaxio caught the creature on the left leg, before he could pull the rope taut; Urudu had slashed the rope, making the hook useless. Vernu fired an exploding ball at its forehead, but Urudu moved faster and a sword flicked it away, blowing the fish statue to bits. Bruno ran up the stairs of a temple, and Urudu followed.

When he reached the top, he swung on a rope and kicked the monster and it wobbled. With its back to Vernu, she fired, and the creature fell, smashing on the ground. After finding nothing in the temple, they picked the onions and chives. It was a long ordeal and after Galaxio had whistled Zilli; he flew for two days, returning them to The Sibell.

Ali smiled when he saw Cilistinu piloting the ship, and they hugged.

"Promise me you are well now."

"The doctor gave me a clean bill of health yesterday," He said thumbing over his shoulder. Vernu and Valentina joined them and they had a group hug.

"How about that rematch you threatened me with?"

"Not yet, old man," He said, waving his sword away. "I need to rest!" And then he went down the stairs to his bedroom.

Chapter Thirteen

Vernu's quill checked off another ingredient. Ali yawned and stretched his arms. He grabbed the red apple from the bowl next to his mother and munched.

"You know that's from the killer apple trees on Zalon?"

He coughed and spat the fruit out. She laughed, and so did her staff.

"Hilarious!" he said, unimpressed.

"There wasn't any poisonous fruit left after our battle." "These are safe."

"Please don't do that again."

"Aww, where's your sense of fun," She said in mother-to-baby voice and waggling his cheeks.

"Get off, mum, you're embarrassing me," He said, waving her hands away.

"Okay, okay," She said, holding up her hands in mock surrender. "What do you know about the next mission?" She said, circling the word "Chorizo"

"Well, first things first, are Tina and Stinu, joining us?"

"As far as I know, they are both fit. I think Stinu is yearning to get out in 'The field.'

"That's convenient, because some terrain on Urshai has fields. The fields are where the wild boars are and they good for chorizo," He finished his apple, and threw the core in the bin. "Our journey will take us across jungles and forests."

"Are you worried about Stinu joining us?"

"I worried about Galaxio and Bruno joining us, but they are capable. Galaxio especially surprised me. He is good in a crisis and handy with a rope too."

"What made you doubt his abilities?"

"I am not sure. I will need to talk to Tina and see what she thinks. I'll find her."

The tongs fizzled as Tina dipped them in a bucket of water. Tina had her back to him. When she noticed him she lifted her visor and smiled. Black oily smears covered her face and her brown hair was messy.

"Ah, Ali, good to see you!" She said, taking off her visor and placing it next to the tongs. "I have finished a new batch of exploding balls. We should have enough now."

"Good, they proved effective in battle. Tina, can I ask you a question?"

"Sounds interesting," She said, with a look of wonder.

"It's about Galaxio. What can you tell me about him?"

"Well, until recently, he was a reluctant assistant. I should have guessed; the clue is in his name."

"What do you mean?"

"His name means: romantic person, not a great lover of danger!"

Ali laughed. "That is ironic, as most of your missions are dangerous."

"But there's more to him than that. He's a pro."

"How long has he been your assistant?"

"Oh, about two years."

"When did you notice a change in him?"

"Probably when he started reading the book." Ali stood and paced about, rubbing his chin.

"So this is a recent change, just a matter of weeks?"

"Yes that's right."

"Interesting, very interesting," Ali said.

"We have another link to this book of yours. Did he say anything to you about it?"

"He did!"

Ali leaned in closer. "What did he say?"

"He is sure the book is full of wisdom. He wants to read more."

"What if you could invent a machine that makes loads of copies?" he asked.

"Amazing, that would save my achy hand," She said rubbing her left wrist. "I bet the Dyidians made one."

"So there isn't a way for you to make one then?"

"I have a few ideas, but I have a lot to learn. We would need a manual or a blueprint. Maybe we will get lucky on this but I am not putting anyone else in danger."

"I appreciate that. We've faced enough danger and it isn't over yet. I mean, what if…." He stopped himself from saying if they had killed her father.

"What do you mean?"

"Oh, it doesn't matter. I must practice," He said, picking up his Nimcha and taking the stairs two at a time.

"He didn't die, and neither did anyone else," She said to herself.

Chapter Fourteen

Seven rough days at sea ended when they weighed anchor off the coast of Urshai. They stationed The Sibell a mile from shore, so rocks wouldn't destroy it. Skilfully, Stinu guided the rowing boat between the rocks and they secured it. There were few men that could have done it.

Treading carefully past rocks, the warm white sand welcomed them. There were palm and coconut trees and exotic flowers. Somewhere a parrot squawked, but everybody was on guard. Beautiful islands didn't fool them, they were still dangerous. Attentively, they proceeded into the jungle. The dusty path was a question mark, and it curved round the island. In the background; they saw a large purple mountain, looking down on them like a god.

Lush vegetation and the sound of insects and rustling leaves surrounded them. When they reached the tip, the path veered left, and they saw monkeys swinging from trees. Everyone knew what to do. Ali and Stinu checked the trees whilst Vernu and Tina checked the ground. Suddenly, Stinu stopped them with his hand.

"Stand still and look up there," He said, whispering and pointing to an enormous spider.

Its body was the size of a cow, and droplets of saliva dribbled from its jaws. It shifted position, and six spots flashed on its abdomen. It turned again, and they saw six more. They were silver blue, as if they charged the spider with electricity.

There was no escape, so the gang tried to creep past, but it saw them. Hissing, it dropped to the floor using its web. Weapons drawn, they faced it. Tina got stung, and the creature cocooned her with webbing.

Chapter Fifteen

The heat separated the precious metal from the copper. Then in a pestle, Clepta ground herbs to obtain acid and then he mixed it with salt and boiling water. He submerged the object in the water; the acid removed the copper oxide. He left it too cool then he reheated and poured it into disc shaped moulds. When the discs had cooled but were still pliable, he removed them from the moulds and stamped one side with a seal. Then he turned the disc over and stamped the other side with a different seal. He leant back and smiled. "Are you coming to bed, now darling? You have been up awfully late." Beatrice said. Clepta looked up. His wife was standing in the doorway dressed in a full length nightie. The light from her candle accentuated her beautiful face.

"I'll be right with you Bea, just finishing up".

"Okay, don't be too much longer" she said, and he heard the stairs creek as she went back to bed. After he had finished he changed into his pyjamas and slid in next to her.

"Are you happy with this batch?" she asked
"Yes, very happy".

***

Tina lay there unconscious, bound like a caterpillar waiting to hatch.

"Argh" Stinu shouted, launching himself at the titan. His sword clashed against the creature's jaws. Arrow flew from Vernu's bow as she tried to bring the beast down. Wounded, their enemy still fought but it pinned Stinu between two trees with its web.

Ali slashes a leg, and it toppled. Then he ran and plunged his sword into its belly. A deafening cry came from the animal and Ali rolled before it collapsed.

Hacking through the webbing with his Jambiya, he freed Tina and her father, but Tina remained unconscious.

Vernu reached into her bag and pulled out a vial containing a light brown liquid. Tilting her head forward, Vernu dabbed Tina's lips to the vial, but she didn't respond.

A gentle prising of the lips and the liquid went down her throat. With a gasp, the young woman awoke. They helped her to her feet, but she was very weak.

After scooping her up, Stinu carried her to a wooden shack, and Ali made a fire. Shivers ran through her and her forehead went hot and cold, aftereffects of the spider venom.

Vernu prepared beef stew. Ali asked Stinu to help lift the fallen monster, and he retrieved his sword. After wiping the blade, Ali sheathed his weapon.

"Thanks for doing that. I know it's only a sword, but it belonged to my father and I want to look after it."

"Don't mention it. She looks okay. Spider venom takes two days to wear off. Besides, I needed something to stop me worrying about Tina."

"You said she would be all right in a day or two."

"Yes, and she will, but that doesn't stop me worrying about her.

"I worried about you after that harpy attack, and that dream you had."

"What dream was that?"

"I was wondering if you would remember." Ali retold the dream, and the colour drained from Stinu's face. "What's wrong, you don't look too good."

Ali tried to get up, but his legs buckled and Stinu helped him sit. Ali grabbed hold of Stinu's long-sleeved tee shirt.

"I think we must pray.

"Okay," He said, not knowing what to say.

"Lord of Jeremiah, I am frightened by Stinu's dream and I feel I cannot avoid it. I pray you will give me the strength to deal with what's ahead of me, Amen."

"Amen," Stinu repeated. "Let's get inside, it's getting dark."

Ali nodded, and they left the sinister jungle behind. And then the half-moon appeared as a menacing slit from behind a cloud.

Upon entering, they saw Tina shivering, so Vernu placed another blanket on her. She was talking and rocking, trying to keep warm, but she didn't look as pale as she had. She smiled when she saw them, but she looked tired. Stinu hugged her.

"I think you should go to sleep, Tina," He said with concern. After finding a bed, they laid out blankets for her and another blanket for a pillow. He kissed her forehead and wiped a stray hair from her face, and then he sat next to Ali who warmed himself in front of the fireplace.

"Bruno is a good guy, what a warrior!"

"Yes. I picked all of my men myself. Some are hard to find, others are easier."

"Was Bruno easy to find?"

"No, he volunteered, but he was nothing special to begin with, just an average young boy who started off as ship hand, until he became Sus's student."

"Who was Sus?"

"Sus was the greatest warrior I ever had the privilege of working with, and he saw something in Bruno. He taught him everything he knew."

"Wow, that's amazing!"

"It wasn't a rose garden for Bruno. He was a sweet-natured boy, very polite, but combat made him cry and occasionally he vomited."

"What happened to Sus?"

Stinu sighed. "He died a warrior's death, in battle."

Ali puffed his cheeks and let out a sigh. "I'm sure I don't have to tell you, it's part of the life we choose."

"Ain't that the truth," and they clinked their flagons together.

"To Sus," Stinu said

"To Sus," Ali echoed clashing their flagons once again.

"What is interesting is Bruno's response to his mentor's death."

"I am guessing he didn't take it well." Stinu shook his head, gasped and wiped beer froth from his beard.

"He was your age, fifteen, and he had been training with Sus for six years."

"They killed his parents when his village got ransacked. I found him after he hid for three days and took him aboard The Sibell. Sus was like a father to him.

"When he heard the terrible news, he withdrew to his quarters for a day, and then he asked me to take him to Timun. (Raetic for calm) He asked if he could stay there for three days. I agreed, provided we remained anchored off the coast. He accepted, and he entered the island a boy and came off it a man."

"You know we need to visit Timun on this trip, don't you?" Ali said.

"Yes, I do. Are you thinking of asking him

to join us on Timun?" Stinu said. "If you think we need him. I think we should ask him and see what he wants to do."

"Okay. I don't think it's as calm as it used to be." Stinu said

"Really? I thought it was just a beach and few clifftops."

"I heard a deadly tribe had moved in there and specialised in crossbreeding animals." Stinu said.

"We'll find out soon enough, and I have faith in us and our abilities."

"I think we need to try and get Khalid off our backs," Ali said.

"What do you have in mind?" "Well, he's a king, right?"

"Last time I looked, yes."

"Where are you going with this, boy?" Stinu said, sounding agitated.

"Kings care about power and wealth. I already think he has too much power, but if we could find something valuable, we might be able to get him to leave Tarnuz alone." Stinu smiled.

"You are smarter than you think Ali. I think that's exactly what we need to do! I am sure we can set aside some of the spoils for King Khalid. "I will keep my eyes open!" Ali said, and then he grinned.

"That's the spirit!" Stinu groaned as he got to his feet and stretched his back.

"I am off to bed. Goodnight Vernu good night Ali."

"Goodnight," They both replied.

"I think we will have many more adventures left with those two," Vernu said.

"I agree, and I think they are very good at what they do. I really trust them now."

Vernu looked surprised, and then she smiled. Then they went to bed too.

A rock smashed through the roof, waking them. An enormous bird's-eye appeared in the opening and looked at them.

"Quick, in here," Stinu said to Tina, waving her into the cellar, whilst he held the hatch open. They made sure she was comfortable, and then they prepared to fight.

A minute passed, and they heard a familiar squawk. It was Zilli. There were sounds of wings flapping on the roof and birds struggling. With trembling hands, Stinu found a crow in a cage.

"Lord, deliver us from evil," He said and kissed the bird and released the animal, asking The Sibell for help. The crow took to the air quickly and help would arrive soon. The Roc which was the name of the enemy bird, had pinned Zilli down, and Stinu threw his spear at and it pierced its thigh, letting go of their feathered ally. Zilli gained height and made an arrow formation, dropping his head, aiming the spike on his helmet at the Roc's neck. He sped towards the monster and the monster toppled to its death. Zilli fluttered down next to them and they saw a huge wound on his side. Tina made a salve for Zilli, but she was too weak to give it to him. Vernu and Ali tended to him, and Stinu welcomed the reinforcements. Bruno ran around looking at the skies.

"These animals are soaking," Stinu said, examining the horses the crew had brought with them.

"We thought you wouldn't just need manpower, we thought you would need the horses too," Galaxio said.

"Well, you're not wrong, but the jagged shoreline concerned me. I thought it might frighten them."

"We had to steer them carefully, but we got here and we injured none of them."
Stinu nodded. "Okay, thanks."

"It's Roc breeding season, so I can guarantee this fiend will have a mate. We need to head for that purple mountain and slay the female and its eggs," Stinu said, briefing his men. "Galaxio, fly with Zilli and nurse him back to health. He will take you to his homeland."

"As you wish, Sir. I will take good care of him and I will see you when I get back."

"Good man. I pray you have a safe trip." With that, Galaxio boarded the bird, and they flew off to safety. "I want the rest of you to guard us until Tina is well enough to travel again, which should only be two more days. We shall dine on Roc," He said, looking at Vernu, who borrowed Ali's sword to carve up the enormous bird. Ali enlisted a couple of Stinu's men to help.

Two days passed, and Tina was back to normal. Three days traveling through fields, forests and rocky terrain, brought them to the Roc nest. Men plunged their swords into the eggs and soon after that, the angry mother returned. The bird gripped Bruno by the shoulders and carried him away, but crew pulled him to safety.

Several spears were thrown, and the beast flew away, but a spear skewered it, knocking it off balance. It collided with rocks and rolled down the mountain like a feathered boulder. They set fire to the nest, and then they climbed down the mountainside. After four hours, they reached the bottom and set up camp.

In the morning, they rose early and after breakfast; they resumed their quest.

Nadal watched them from his tree hideout. When they had turned their backs, he got down and found a Pangolin nosing around in the dust. Once again, he took out his purple powder and poured it on the animal, muttering a fresh set of words. A short time later, the creature creaked like leather and it grew. There was a spitting sound and spikes appeared on its tail, making it look like a large mace. Its eyes changed from brown to purple, and Nadal smiled before he returned to his hiding place. After sighting the adventurers, the pangolin charged them.

Bruno stood his ground, but the spiky tail swatted him like a bluebottle, knocking him out. Men threw spears, but the creature rolled itself into a ball, sending them flying like skittles. The four heroes bunched together, and the beast breathed heavily, its scaly armour rising and falling with each breath. Balling up again, it rolled towards them and they dived in different directions.

Tina saw a small crack in the ground, large enough for a man. She threw a rock, hitting the monster's back. It spun round and charged towards her. Wedging herself into the gap, she held her spear high. The pangolin tried to stop itself, but it was too late and it was impaled on the tip. Its legs moved frantically before it was still. With, a few grunts and swear words they lifted the pangolin off her, pulling her to safety. And then the pangolin shrank before their eyes.

"This wasn't the animal's natural size. Something or someone brought about its change," Tina said. As she spoke, she saw Nadal emerge from his hiding place and watched him drop some powder and an orange smoke cloud took him away.

They gathered everyone, and they sent a few injured men back to the ship. Bruno was fine, but it disappointed him he would miss out on the action.

It was lunchtime, so Vernu started a fire and prepared some food.

"I have had a feeling we were being pursued," Tina said.

"When did you suspect?" Ali said.

"I think it was when we collected the olives. I have never seen Sorapis that size before, and shortly after, we came across many weird and wonderful monsters. Now the king's vizier is here!" Her face was red and her brown eyes blazed. He hadn't seen her as angry as this before.

"Do you think the king sent him or do you think he works alone?"

"I really hope he is working on his own, because if the king is behind this, I feel war with King Khalid is inevitable!"

Ali puffed his cheeks. "Do you have any other suggestions?"

"A few. He could manipulate the King."

"Okay, let's assume that's what's going on here. How would he do that?"

"If it was me, I would slip potions into his drink. It would need to be tasteless so the King wouldn't know anything and it would need to fool the royal taster," Then she jumped to her feet with a wild look on her face. "That's it! I am pretty certain that's exactly what's going on! She clicked her fingers. "Nadal is using a mind control drug on the King and the royal taster is also under its spell!" "Oh, this is clever, brilliant," She said, and stopped pacing.
Ali jumped to his feet, and he also snapped his fingers without meaning to.

"And with my mum out of the picture, no one is there to monitor the food as it leaves the kitchen!"

"I think you are right and I wouldn't be surprised if all the catering staff is under its control too!"

"What do you propose we do?"

"I think we need to carry on with the mission and confront Nadal. We can't go back to Tarnuz, as we don't know how many people it affects. I need to get hold of his potions, and then

I will need to test them to find out which one is the mind control drug."

Ali folded his arms and turned his back, and then he stared at the ground. She went to him and lightly touched his shoulder, and he flinched.

"What's wrong Ali, did I say something wrong?"

He turned to face her.

"You know when you have a dream, and it felt real?"

"Yes, I know what you mean."

"Sometimes it's a pleasant dream and you can't wait for it-and then other times it's a bad dream and you don't want it to happen."

She nodded.

"I know your father was unwell, but I think his dream/nightmare is real."

Tina had an idea.

"You must allow yourself to be captured." "I need to find an antidote for the King. I need to analyse Nadal's potions."

"Tina, this is pure speculation. You have no proof and I can't put myself at risk, based on a guess I can't believe you want me to volunteer. I am disposable to you," He said, striding a horse and galloping away from her.

"Ali I'm sorry," She yelled, waving her arms to get him to come back, but it was too late.

Chapter Sixteen

After five days they caught up with Ali. They found the ashes of a campfire. Scattered around the clearing there were thorn bushes. One had a piece of red cloth attached to it, matching his trousers. There were also droplets of blood marking a trail back to the fire.

"The coals are still warm," Stinu said, investigating the embers. "He can't be far away."

As he finished speaking, they all heard the sounds of a commotion. Swords drawn, they ran in the direction of the noise.

Tree imps surrounded Ali. He thrashed at them with his sword, but his wounded hand made him clumsy. They were small, but there were two hundred of them. They carried him away on a sea of hands.

***

Whilst Clepta was away, Bea inspected his handy work. They had met at work and romance quickly started and they married in the spring. That was five years ago.

This batch is different from the normal batches. She thought.

Looking around her husband's work bench she found a letter written in Nadal's handwriting. It read: *further to your visit with Kati and his brother, I trust you have everything you need to carry out the next part of our plan. I look forward to hearing from you and you will be rewarded handsomely for your efforts.*

Yours sincerely,

Nadal.

Hot tears streamed down Beatrice's face as she grabbed Clepta's quill and a piece of parchment.

Clepta selected a dozen red roses from the florist's stall in the market place and asked him to wrap them. He paid and whistled as he walked back to his house.

A cool morning breeze blew across his face and bird song lilted towards him as he approached his house, a short distance from the market. He turned the key in the door, open the door.

"Bea, I have bought you your favourites, red roses." He said, and found the secateurs and snapped the ends. He filled a vase of water from the well bucket and placed the flowers on the kitchen table. He looked over at his work bench and saw a note. He went over and opened it. It was written in Bea's neat writing.

My dearest Clepta.

I have warned you on many occasions that Nadal is a very dangerous man and cannot be trusted. It is clear to me you are unable to stand up to him and you happy to do his bidding. I can't live with someone who chooses a criminal over his wife. I have asked you to choose him or me. It is clear you have chosen him. If you change your mind, I am staying at my mother's.

Bea.

Clepta slid to the ground clutching her note.

"No, Bea, I am such a fool!" He yelled, his lips quivering and he started crying uncontrollably.

***

Ali looked like a crowd surfer. Vernu looked helpless as they carried her son away, and the imps moved further into the jungle. She sank to the floor and started weeping. Tina sat next to her and they cuddled.

"We need to keep up the search, captain," Bruno said.

"I agree. Tina, what do we know about tree imps?"

"I thought you could tell me that!"

"I don't know everything. I have never come across them before. I have heard about them."

"They are pretty harmless. Unless you have a shiny object. It doesn't matter if it's worthless. They don't normally carry someone off like that." "I think they are working with Nadal. It's the only thing that makes sense."

"We must stop him, we must get Ali back," Stinu said.

***

The flame burnt his torso, and he yelled. His arms ached from the rope binding cutting his wrists.

"Ah, Alessandro. Glad you're awake," Nadal said, grinning like a hyena.

He saw they had tied him to a wooden beam in a tree house. He was at least three metres from the floor.

"There are nicer ways of waking someone up, you know."

"This is true, but then, where's the fun in that," he smiled again, revealing yellow teeth. A black jewel glowed in place of the right canine. He probably lost a fight in a tavern.

"I know you're up to something Nadal, and I aim to find out what it is."

This time, the villain laughed. It was as if he had plunged into an icy lake and Ali shivered.

"You have no idea what you are talking about, and you have no proof of any wrong doing. You have seriously misjudged me. I have Tarnuz eating out of my hand," He said, turning his back and his dark blue robe swished as he walked.

Tina was right. Here goes!

He puffed out his chest. "I know you are using a mind control potion, on the king and the entire country,"

Nadal stopped stirring his cauldron and faced him.

"I doubt you concluded this by yourself!" He roared, spittle flying from his jaws, some of it dribbled down his black and grey beard. His pupils became tiny black dots of terror.

"I can see you are the brawn, but I suspect the little girl is the brains," He said turning back to his cauldron. He stirred it and the liquid belched, and then the tree house smelt of cheesy feet. Ali gagged.

"Anyway, you can't do a thing when you're hanging around like that, can you?" He said, walking over and pushing Ali's stomach. Ali swung, but this time, he vomited all over Nadal's dark blue sheik hat. The boy laughed.

"I think you had better get changed. Besides, Tina maybe smarter than me, but I am not stupid," And he jumped to the ground Jambiya drawn.

"How did you do that?"

"I could tell you, but then where's the fun in that?"

The two men circled each other and Nadal swiped at Ali's throat, but Ali was too fast bent out of the way.

Before they continued fighting, they saw smoke rising from the ground. Nadal rushed to the window, and he saw the crew fitting the imps in the blazing jungle. After cursing, he grabbed a vine and slid to the ground. Finding his Equomel, he whacked the beast and left.

Ali gathered up Nadal's book and as many potions as he could. If he couldn't find the mind control potion, he would have wasted his time. Then he used the same vine Nadal used and landed softly. Vernu held out her hand and he jumped onto her horse. They galloped away as the jungle burnt.

They sheltered in an old palace. Faded tapestries hung from the walls. Gold candlesticks were covered in cobwebs and the dining table had wood worm. The staircase had stairs missing. The holes in the marble floor made the royal crest difficult to see.

This could be Tarnuz if we don't succeed. Tina thought, and she shuddered.

"It looks like this was a once the palace of a Dyidian King."

Ali said, looking up from an old book he found.

"You speak Dyidian now?" Tina said, peering over his shoulder. He slammed the book, and the dust made her cough.

"No, I could make out the word Dyidian and the pictures told the rest!"

"Let me see," but he pulled the book away, and then he handed it to her, smiling.

"Pig!" She said, poking her tongue out.

He looked at another extract of the old book.

"It turns out you were right about Nadal and the whole mind control thing."

"Sorry, are you okay? I forgot to ask how you were. Is the salve working?"

He touched the bandage on his chest. He was still tender, but the coolness of the salve soothed his discomfort.

"Thanks for asking. I'll live. How do you think Zilli is doing?"

"It was a nasty injury but, he will make a full recovery. Just like I have faith in you too. What did Nadal tell you?"

"Well, I just came right out with it."

"What happened?"

"He got furious. That guy is terrifying!"

"No doubt."

"He accused me of being all brawn and you were the brains."

"Well, he got that right!" she said.

He tried to play punch her, but the pain stopped him.

"I apologise. I should be more sensitive."

He raised his eyebrows.

"Don't look at me like that!"

"He admitted it, but we can't stop him yet. We need to finish our mission."

"That's true. When I get back to The Sibell, I will need to make a large batch of antidote."

"Don't worry, I will help you."

"Thanks. Aren't you worried I will be mean to you?"

"I can be pretty mean, too."

"That's true."

"Oi! I may insult myself, you haven't earnt the right yet."

"I guess," She said, and they smiled.

"Nadal was making this vile concoction. It smelt like your dad's feet."

"Eww," She said, wrinkling her nose and laughing. He laughed too. As quickly as her smile arrived, it disappeared again.

"What's the matter Tina?"

"I struggle with the potions I use."

"In what way?" Ali said

"In the old book they trust The Lord for their healing and I make potions not only to heal, but to do other things too."

"I read The Lord enabled people to find healing by looking at a bronze Sorapis on a staff. If you use your potions, give thanks to God." "How do you think people viewed glasses when they were first invented? They probably thought it was sorcery. I think we could say the same for many inventions. And yet most of them are normal now." Ali said.

"It would appear you are not all brawn after all!"

"I have never taken advice from deranged old men in dark robes, and I will not start now!"

"Good for you," She said, playfully punching his bicep. "You made me think. I should give The Lord the glory. It's easier saying The Lord than The Lord of Jeremiah."

"Yes, and the Israelites came before Jeremiah and they called him Lord." He replied.

"I think we should too. It looks like they really knew him." She said.

"Maybe we will, too."

"I hope so."

"I do too."

"I am not a Dyidian expert, but what I have seen, it looks like they believed in The Lord." She said.

"I think they believed in him enough to want to translate his book."

"We need to find more of the book, but I can't help thinking we could probably live right by The Lord with everything we have so far." He offered.

"Yes, but it would be amazing to find the rest."

"How right you are!"

"I am sure we will find more when the time is right." He replied.

"After fighting all the beasts we have fought, puzzles we've solved, the most fascinating thing about it all is this dusty old book!"

"I know it's a mystery that needs solving. And that's exciting!" She said, looking thoughtful

"I think I need to skip the rest of this island and recover on the ship," He said, wincing as he moved.

"If you're sure."

"Yes, I think it would be for the best. I want to read the book." Getting up gingerly, he found one of the old sea dogs and chatted briefly. They both went back to the ship.

***

After breakfast, Vernu's poached eggs, they headed out. After, a three-hour walk, they disturbed foraging wild boar. When they saw them they charged.

Bruno slit the hog's throat. It squealed and died. Stinu drove his sword into a swine's forehead. Vernu felled another with her bow and spear welding sailors killed the last one.

They carved the boars, packed them, and sent the horses back to the ship.

"Wow, you have been busy!" Tina said when she entered her lab. Ali found the ingredients she would need for the antidote. After three hours, the remedy was ready. "Now we need a test subject for the antidote."

"Bruno!" They said at the same time.

Vernu gave Bruno his favourite dish, and he tucked in. He drank mead and had no idea what was happening. The youngsters sniggered behind his back and then went above deck. They laughed and Tina waved her legs in the air. Ali sat down, clutching his chest. After a few minutes, they regained their composure.

"How long will it be for the drug to work?"

"It should be in his system within forty-five minutes."

"I can't wait!" he said, rubbing his hands together.

"Let me have a look at the burn." She unwrapped the bandage, and the injury looked better. She reapplied the bandage, and he thanked her. "How many items are left on the list?"

"Do you mean the royal meal?"

She nodded.

"Let me see. Red and yellow peppers," He said, and counted them on his fingers. "Garlic, paprika, saffron, bay leaves and giant lobster makes seven."

"Wait; did you just say giant lobster?"

"Yep!"

"Oh, brother. I don't like the sound of that at all!"

"I didn't want to mention it yet. It's last on the list and it's close to Tarnuz. I thought we'd get smelly fish on feast day."

"I thank you for being considerate. When you say giant lobster how big is it?" Her voice went up an octave.

"Oh, only fifteen metres."

"Fifteen metres?" She said, gulping.

"I shouldn't worry. You don't have to fight it if you don't want to."

"What because I'm a girl?"

"No, I didn't mean that. I think we should see if our patient is ready."

"Yes, we should check on him, but we'll discuss this later," She said, glaring at him.

Bruno sat rigid, arms placed on the table, a vacant look on his face.

Tina waved a hand in front of his face, no reaction.

"He's ready. Bruno, stand up,"

He stood up.

"Stand on one leg."

He followed the command.

"Oh, we are going to have so much fun with this," He said rubbing his hands. "Bruno, cluck like a chicken."

The poor sailor obeyed and flapped his arms. He squatted and pretended to lay an egg.

Ali laughed until his sides hurt.

"Right, that's enough!" "We need to give him the cure now." She said, giving Bruno the antidote.

"You're unbelievable, Ali. Can't you see how dangerous this draft is?"

"Ah, come on Tina, its harmless fun!"

"This is not harmless, far from it!" "Nadal has been controlling Tarnuz for a while."

"Okay, supposing you're right, why haven't we been affected?"

"That is a good question and I don't have the answer to it, yet."

"Look, I meant nothing by it. We have all been under tremendous pressure lately and I just saw it as a bit of fun, that's all."

"Get upstairs," She shouted, pointing at the staircase.

"Okay, Okay, I'm going."

She circled him and huffed.

"Do you remember our conversation yesterday?"

"Which one exactly?"

"The one where I doubted I was doing the right thing with using potions?"

"Ah, I see where this is going. Yes, I do. I am sorry," He said, looking at the floor.

She lent on the side of the boat next to him. She took a deep breath.

"I believe the Lord has given us gifts." "But I think Nadal wields evil over the King." "The Lord gives and Nadal tries to take away."

Ali looked shocked.

"Now you can see that this is very serious!"

"You don't have to tell me twice. I think if you use knowledge to make drafts- potions sounds sinister to me- and use them to do good and you give The Lord glory, I think you will be fine."

"I couldn't agree more. I think I won't make a draft until I have prayed about it first."

"That's a wonderful idea. You never know, The Lord may reveal a recipe to you in a dream or something."

"That's very true, or show us were we can find a recipe."

"I think that is another thing to get excited about! Think of all the things we could achieve, all the lives we could change, all the people we could save."

"One thing at a time. We need to concentrate on making enough antidote for Tarnuz first."

"Yeah, and then we will need to get it into the water supply."

"I am glad you understand the urgency, but I need to test Bruno more."

"What sort of tests?"

"I need to find out if longer exposure means the remedy takes longer to work."

"That's a good point."

"We won't give Bruno anymore tests today, we'll resume tomorrow."

"I'll tell you one thing, Tina."

"What's that?"

"Nadal is going to be mad about losing his book. Don't be surprised if he wants it back."

"Well, when that time comes; I'll be ready for him."

"I hope you are, but we'll be ready to back you up, if you need us to."

"Thanks. I need all the help I can get. And why can't I fight the lobster?"

"Oh, not that again! Truthfully, I may not fight it either. It all depends on how I heal," He said, rubbing his belly.

"You will probably have a little scaring, but the bandage will come off in a few more days."

"Good to know."

***

She ran tests on Bruno and found the potion didn't work after five days. After this, the crew gathered around the table in the map room and Ali and Stinu laid out the plan they had for returning Tarnuz to normal.

"We need to put it at the back of our minds. We must focus on our current aim, getting the remaining parts of the meal." "But we will go over the plan in greater detail later on." Stinu said, smiling and looking at his crew.

"Is everyone clear?"

"Yes," they all chorused.

Six more days at sea and they spied the next island. After lowering the horses into the sea, the four adventurers led their animals to the shore. When they crossed the beach, they trotted along a track. The land was covered with many herbs, but most of them looked brown or withered. It hadn't rained for some time, but the sky was as black as night and the gang would need to take shelter. Although the herbs had seen better days, they could smell oregano, basil, thyme and rosemary. They were herbs that turned food into cuisine.

Vernu dismounted and took as many cuttings as she could.

There was a flash of lightening that forked across the sky, showing a large empty brick house.

"Over there," Stinu said, pointing at the house. "We'll rest here for the night. There should be room inside for the horses, too."

The others looked at him as if he was crazy.

"Look, we will need our horses and I don't want them running off. It should only be for one night."

The others shrugged, and they led their animals inside. They climbed the wooden stairs and went through the door. There were two windows at the front and two at the back. There was a dining room table, some chairs, a stove and a fireplace on the right wall. A staircase was next to the fireplace. The rain and hail drummed loudly on the roof as it pelted the building.

"It looks like you found this house just in time," Vernu said.

"Yes, it looks sturdy enough," Stinu said, bouncing on the floorboards and looking at the ceiling.

Ali fed the horses, and they seemed happy enough, just as grateful as the humans to be safe from the storm.

When Vernu's crusty white bread was ready, Ali toasted two slices in front of the fire. Once the second slice was done, he slid it off the tongs on to his plate. He covered both in butter then he spread yeast extract on too. Tina covered hers with Vernu's strawberry jam. They sat opposite each other at a wooden table, the kind you find in tavern garden.

"Eww, do you really eat that stuff," She said, wrinkling her nose.

"No, I'm going to use it to seal up the cracks in this place. Of course I'm going to eat it."

"*Sorry for being so stupid*!"

"I get that it's not everyone's cup of tea, but I really like it."

"Okay, fair enough. How did you feel when you were kidnapped by Nadal?" She said, changing the subject.

"I suppose I should have been petrified because of your father's dream, but I wasn't. I just had an overwhelming urge to get the truth out of Nadal. I didn't think about being afraid, but that might have had something to do with the pain I was feeling," He said, sliding his empty plate away.

"You've changed, and I think it might have something to do with the old book."

"I may have changed, but you are still the intellectual hypocrite you've always been!"

"I beg your pardon!" And whilst she wasn't looking, he swiped her toast and ate it, with a smug grin on his face. "Now that's just rude. I said beg your pardon."

"I heard you the first time."

"How am I a hypocrite?"

136

"When we were testing the antidote on Bruno, you were kicking your legs in the air and laughing as much as I was, then you bang on about how serious mind control is and blah, blah, blah. Little miss high and mighty."

She got up and smashed his plate. Then she stormed upstairs and slammed one of the bedroom doors.

Calmly, he reached for the rest of the loaf and cut two more slices. He walked over to the fire. Even though the crackling of the flames was loud, he could still hear Tina sobbing upstairs. When the toast was ready he spread them with butter and jam and took them to her room.

With a soft tap, he knocked on the door and left the plate for her to discover. There was a pause, and then the door opened and he could hear her munching, ravenously. Stinu sat next to him.

"You have a lot to learn about women, young man," He said, warming his palms in front of the flames, copying Ali.

"Is this 'The don't talk to my daughter like that, speech'?"

"Come to think of it, you have a lot to learn about how to talk to *people*."

"She's no better."

"I am not saying she is. Sometimes the pair of you could do with being a little less teenage."

"But right here, that's who I am, that's who we both are."

"That's very true, but you both need to show each other more respect. If you feel yourself losing your temper, think about the bigger picture; the freedom of Tarnuz. We all have a part to play in keeping our country peaceful, it's very humbling."

"I suppose."

"I think we should keep both of you apart on the next trip. I think you should consider the good things about each other. I'll leave you to put out the fire. I see your mother as retired and I need my bed, too," He said, yawning and the stairs creaked as he went up to his bedroom.

Ali sat for ten minutes, and then he put the fire out and went to bed.

After breakfast, they rode on the river path which fed into a ravine. Soon after this they came face to face with a Sarcosuchus, a giant crocodile.

"Stinu, you and Ali take the horses up that hill, away from this monster. Tina and I know what to do," Vernu said, taking control.

Surprised, but also not wanting any harm to come to the horses, Stinu helped Ali get the animals to safety. From their point of safety, they heard the women grunt and yah as they fought the creature, and they could hear the snapping of jaws and thrashing in the water, and then there was silence. The men tried to peer around the bush, but the foliage was too dense. Tina whistled.

"Ali, I have a job for you," she yelled.

He slid down the slope disturbing the orange earth and walked towards Tina. She held out her Jambiya to him. Looking at the floor he could see the Sarcosuchus was trussed up like a spit roast.

Ignoring her dagger, he drew his Nimcha and plunged it in to the reptile's head, twisting the blade until it died. With a gaze of steel fixed on Tina, he wiped his blade on his trousers. Turning in silence, he went back to help Stinu bring the horses down.

"He doesn't like being mocked," Vernu said.

"I wasn't mocking him."

"Are you sure about that?"

"Yes. I thought the dagger would do the job."

Vernu laughed. "There's no way that little knife would penetrate the beast's skull. You have a lot to learn about combat, Tina," She said, and then she straddled her horse.

Ali convinced the others to go back to the house.

"I am still tender, anyway. Have some fun," He said, sitting down and unrolling a section of the book, and then he bit into a dark red apple. They left him supplies.

"I'll send for reinforcements. We need more help now," Stinu said.

Stinu scribbled the coordinates on a note and sent a crow. Time passed and Bruno and his men arrived. There weren't enough horses, so they doubled up. They passed temple ruins and sheltered in a house in an abandoned village. Stinu opened the top-floor window and watched the bright orange sunset.

Crickets and bullfrogs signalled the end of the day. After a while, Stinu heard large flapping wings. Looking up, he could see a humanoid shape with bat wings and a green horn flashed on its head. The monster had three toes on each foot. It was six metres tall.

Grabbing his sword, he ran downstairs and joined the fight. Men threw spears, but the beast covered its body with its wings and the weapons bounced off.

Some of Vernu's arrows stuck out of its furry belly, but they were superficial wounds. It landed on the roof of the house and pulled out the arrows with its beak. It took flight and breathed fire, raising the house to the ground. The crew ran in different directions, but it burnt the dry grass around them. The creature swooped down on Stinu, who tripped on a tree root, and dropped his sword.

***

In the throne room, King Stefano enjoyed the cool fans his servants waved. One stood on the left of the throne and the other on the right. They fanned him with peacock feathers. Just then, King Khalid burst in with his entourage, disturbing the peace.

"What has your merry band of renegades been up to, Stefano? It's been weeks now and they still haven't returned with the ingredients for my feast."

"Dear King Khalid, I received a homing pigeon today saying they have seven items left. It shouldn't be too much longer now."

"Will you open your eyes and pay attention to this very serious matter?"

Stefano did as he asked.

"I know how serious this is. You have rationed my people and prevented trade. I have starving subjects coming to me every day and I can feed them because the store rooms are well stocked, but the supplies will run dry soon. If the king would be so kind as to free us up, I will do everything I can to speed up the adventurers."

King Khalid's face softened a bit.

"Very well, I will make my supplies available to the citizens of Tarnuz, but I will not allow trade ships to come and go until I have had my meal."

"All I am asking is that you feed my people, and that you give my explorers a little more time. I will send a pigeon to them underling how important all of this is and that time is running out."

"Make sure you do and in the meantime, I will relax my hand and allow everyone the food they need, he said clapping his hands and he and his entourage left.

"Thank you gracious King, you are so kind," He said, clicking his fingers and the royal scribe stepped forward.

"Write this," he said, and he dictated the message he wanted to send to the crew. The scribe jotted down the message after he had finished writing. He had the document to the king, who read it then signalled for melted red wax and sealed it with his ring. The letter was attached to the pigeon that had arrived earlier that day and then it was sent back to The Sibell.

Chapter Seventeen

Stepping in front of her father, Tina fired a ball at the fiend and the ball exploded. There was a cracking sound and ice spread over the body of the bat thing. Vernu fired another silver ball at its tummy and the creature fell out the sky, too heavy to fly. It crashed to the ground, making a large trench. Vernu drew her sword and ran up to its head and cut off the glowing horn, and with a final moan, it took its last breath.

"Thank you for your help, ladies, I thought that was the end of me. Then he stopped smiling. "Your son is a monster expert, right?"

Vernu nodded. "What's your point, Stinu?"

"Well, I can't help thinking that it was awfully convenient that he needed a rest when we had to fight bat thing. I think he knew it lived here and he decided to sit this one out!"

"I see, you want to blame my son for not having your back when he isn't here to defend himself. You have a very capable crew, so what's your problem, exactly?" Vernu said taking, deep breathes. Tina stood next to Stinu and frowned at Vernu.

"Why don't we go and get your son and see what he has to say for himself."

"Okay, I will. I'll take Bruno and some men with me."

"Fine, I think that would be the best idea, as I am at a wits end with the pair of you!"

"Oh, I am so sorry your spoilt little daughter doesn't like being put her place!"

"Get out!" He roared, face turning red. Vernu gathered Bruno and some other men and left to retrieve her son.

"You didn't need to yell, dad."

"Maybe not, but she made me see red."

"Yes I can see where he gets his feistiness from."

"I can't guess where you get yours from," He said, winking and then smiling at her. She play punched his arm.

"I am at a loss for words!" She said and they both laughed.

"I think we will all have a little chat when they get back."

"I agree. We have let things get on top of us."

Vernu, Ali and the other men arrived with the horses after everyone else was in bed. Vernu thought it best to try and make peace in the morning. *We have a few more weeks left of this mission and we need to get along.* She thought.

***

Stinu was woken up by the smell of Vernu's porridge. After a stretch and yawn, he padded down the stairs.

"Morning"

"Morning," she replied with a warm smile.

"I think we all need to talk," he said.

"Yes, let's get the children up and see if we can sort it all out."

Ali came down next with a blanket draped over his shoulder and he ladled some porridge into a wooden bowl. Drizzling treacle on to it and then stirring it, and then he sat with his back to the others. Sometime later, Tina came and helped herself to food, after inspecting the labels on the jars, she settled on jam. When they finished, they found a bench in the grass and sat there for a while. A minute passed and then Stinu broke the silence.

"For whatever reason, we have got heated with each other and I want to find out why."

"I feel like everyone's getting at me. I feel like I can't do anything right," Ali said.

"I seem to remember we had a chat about being respectful towards each other, a few days ago."

"There are a few things that I don't like and one of them is hypocrisy and I accused Tina of it."

"I did overreact to that, and I am sorry about that, I really am."

"Apology accepted," He said and smiled and she smiled back.

"There is something I wanted to ask you. Did you know about the bat thing and how dangerous it was?"

"Thanks for the porridge, mum," He said, getting up and running back to the house and Vernu ran after him. Stinu frowned and then looked at Tina and she shook her head.

"I can see why he asked that. If you sat out that battle, I want to know why," Vernu said, placing her hands on his bedposts. He lay with his hands behind his head, staring at the ceiling. He sighed.

"Do you remember that dream I used to have when I was a kid?" Vernu got up, and frowned. Then she closed her eyes to think, trying to recall the memory.

"Yes I do. The bat man! You used to wake up screaming."

"That's him, charming fellow. I did know what kind of wild life we would find here and Stinu was right."

Vernu paced a bit. "We could have all been killed! That was very irresponsible of you. I can't believe you. You need to come to terms with your fears. Come down and apologise, when you're ready. I am very disappointed in you, too," She said, and left slamming the door.

She made four cups of coffee and took them out to the others. By the time the coffee's arrived, Ali appeared looking sorry for himself.

"Sorry. I should have given you the information I had." Then he explained his fears and torments an after much sighing and huffing and puffing, everyone decided to move on.

"Let's pray. Lord, I thank you for Ali, Stinu, Tina and our crew. We all have unique gifts and talents. Help us to be honest with each other and help us to work together. We pray for peace in Tarnuz and we pray that you will keep them safe. Help us succeed in our mission, Amen," Vernu said.

"Amen," They repeated.

"That was a really heart felt prayer, Vernu. I felt like a weight lifted off my shoulders," Tina said, and the others nodded in agreement.

"Thank you. I think the book is about love and think we have lacked a little bit of love towards each other and I think it wouldn't hurt to remember to love each other."

Ali drained his mug and went back to the house.

He opened the door and a young boy stared at him. His light brown hair looked like his mother had placed a bowl on his head and cut round it. His face was dirty and so were the souls of his feet. He grabbed a handful of bread and leapt through one of the glassless windows at the back of the house.

"Hey!" Ali shouted and leapt through the same window. He saw the boy disappear around the side of another house. He followed him around another house and watched as the boy knocked three times on a cellar door. The door opened and two adult hands lifted him over the door jab, then the door was closed again. Ali walked over to the cellar door and he knocked three times too, hoping who ever opened it the first time would open it a second time.

"Go away," a male voice said.

"If you were hiding from the bat thing, my friends and I have slain it." Ali heard numerous voices, male and female, arguing and trying to decide whether to trust the stranger outside.

"Do you have any proof?"

Ali found the horn from the creature in his belt pocket and got it out. His mother had given it to him after she dealt the final blow.

"As a matter of fact, I do."

"Place it at the front of the cellar door and move fifty paces away."

He did as he was told and afterwards, the door opened again and a hand fumbled around and picked it up. It looked like the same hand from before. It was a man's hand. Perhaps the hand belonged to the child's father?

Ali couldn't hear what they were saying and practiced sword play with an imaginary enemy. Not long after, the latch opened and man's head appeared in the opening. He also had the bowl haircut. Pressing his hands either side of him, he hauled himself out of the hole. He extended his hand and pulled out a woman, presumably his wife, who also had the same haircut.

"Thank the Lord for Tarnuz hairdressers," Ali said under his breath.

The son was next and then four more people emerged: a man a woman and two children, a boy and a girl. The girl looked about the same age as bowl boy, but her brother was the youngest. Everyone had bowl haircuts!

Without warning, the first man ran towards Ali and shook his hand so hard; he thought his arm would fall off!

"God be praised. We are eternally grateful for your help. We thought we would never be free from the Van Meter, the monster you destroyed."

"I, err, didn't…

"We had almost given up hope of rescue," said the woman, who was shaking his other hand with force.

The other family stepped forward and Ali was swamped by seven people all showing their gratitude.

"Enough!" He shouted. "Let's start by introducing ourselves, shall we? I am Alessandro, but people call me Ali."

"I am Tarquin," the first man said, pointing at himself. "This is Brenda, my wife and this is my son, Elijah. I'll allow Bryan to introduce his family."

Bryan introduced his wife as Jenny, the boy was known as Adrian and the girl was called Tammy.

"I am honoured to meet you all," Ali said, holding his right hand to his left breast and bowing. "Are you the only survivors?"

"Oh no, we have had our casualties, don't get me wrong. The others are all hiding in their cellars just as we were," Then the children started knocking on the cellar doors of all the houses surrounding them and the area begin to fill with lots of different families, all of them looking at Ali some pointed and some the teenage girls whispered and giggled, and occasionally nudging each other. And then the village turned to look behind him. His mother, Stinu and Tina had come to see where Ali had got to and were surprised to see him in a sea of people. There must have been at least two hundred.

He introduced them and Tarquin invited them into his house. He was the mayor of the village.

"How long had you been under the oppression of the Van Meter?" Vernu asked, before Stinu could. He looked at her with surprise.

"It must be about two months now," He reached over and grabbed Vernu's loaf she had brought for them. The sleeves on his light brown robe slid up revealing very skinny arms and the whole family had sunken eyes and pale skin. She was glad that she and the crew showed up when they did. She poured vegetable soup into the bowls and the family ate noisily, forgetting their manners, but that didn't matter; the quest was bigger than her, than the crew, than King Stefano and even Tarnuz itself. She was convinced they were meant to help others on their journey and that gave her hope.

"How did this creature come about? Was it hibernating and somebody woke it up, was it hungry and it came looking for food?" Stinu asked.

"We aren't sure," Tarquin said, placing his silver spoon in his empty bowl. "We first noticed it when we found our cattle had been slain. At first, we didn't pay attention to it, thinking it was a wolf or bear attack and it only happened at night. Then people started going missing too. And then it started happening during the day as well. It got to the point where everyone was living in fear and we all voted on going into hiding until we could figure out a plan. Eventually, we got enough money together to send for a professional monster hunter. We paid him upfront and we never saw him again. Some of the villagers had given up their life savings."

Stinu and the others reached into their pockets and handed over their coin pouches.

"We'll order the rest of the crew to hand over their pouches too, we have plenty of money."

"Thank you, thank you so much," Tarquin said; his face looked like an excited child at Christmas. "How can we ever repay you?"

"Well, that is very simple. We are on a quest to save our country, Tarnuz. We need to prepare a meal for a King who is threatening to go to war with our King. We have a list of ingredients and we are after red and yellow peppers."

Tarquin's face fell.

"What is the matter?" Vernu asked.

"We can supply you with what you ask, but we need you to rid us off one more monster."

"What monster is this?" Tina asked.

Tarquin sighed and looked down at the table.

"It is a giant toad. We used to travel through the sewers to get to the garden. It was the only way. We had been doing it for years and then all of a sudden people started disappearing. One day, my younger brother went down there and barely escaped with his life. He managed to get back here and tell us everything he could, but the poison had already started to take effect. He died in my arms," He said, and started to sob. His family comforted him.

"Are there any other surprises we need to be aware of down there?" Ali said, hoping there would be more to go on.

"Only rats. I am sure you know how to deal with them," Brenda said, Tarquin was still too upset to talk.

"Have you any thoughts on what its weakness might be?" Vernu asked.

"My brother didn't get that far, I am afraid. Sorry I can't help you more," Tarquin said, managing to regain a little bit of composure.

"I think we should leave right away Tina volunteered."

"Yes. I think these people have suffered enough," Vernu said.

"I don't think I have killed a giant toad before, but there is always a first time," Ali said, swishing his sword.

"Let's go!" Stinu said.

The rest of the crew had gathered outside of Tarquin's house and Stinu filled them in. Some of the men sharpened their swords and they made their way into the dark sewer. The flames from their torches danced on the ceiling of the tunnel, and they could hear running water and the intermittent squeaks of rats and the scurrying of rodent feet. There was a smell of rotting flesh and Stinu turned his flame in the direction of the smell. The light revealed a skeleton dressed in green with a gold medallion around its neck, a sword laid next to its right hand a bow laid next to its left. Stinu went through his pockets and found the villagers money and the contract he signed to kill the toad.

"I think we have found the monster hunter," He said, tossing a large coin pouch at Ali, he caught it.

Ali gulped. "Well, I hope we have better luck than him," he said.

"Have faith, we have fought worse things on this adventure than toads," Tina said.

"Yes and nearly all of them came close to killing us!"

"We know what we're doing," Vernu said.

"So I am assuming this guy didn't?"

He said, pointing at the dead man.

The mouth of the skull was open and it looked like he was laughing at a sick joke. A chill slipped down Ali's spine and he shuddered.

"I think we should push on, don't you?"

They all nodded and carried on with the journey.

The tunnel fanned out in to a clearing and shortly after, they could smell decay and the place was littered with broken bone and shredded clothing.

From a dark corner, two large amphibious eyes fixed themselves on the adventurers.

Moving quickly, despite its bulk, the toad flicked its tongue at them, slamming a crew member to the ground, he lay unconscious. The toad belched and green bile spewed from its mouth, and people coughed and spluttered.

Vernu and Tina fell to their knees and then they collapsed. Enraged, Stinu and Ali hacked, parried and rolled. More bile flowed and Stinu threw his torch at the bile, and it caught on fire.

After writhing and hopping, trying to put out the flames, the toad's eyes rolled in their sockets and the toad died, its tongue lying limp in its mouth.

Stinu and Ali helped the ladies to their feet, but they were still woozy from the attack.

In front of them was a slope which led to a gate that had a disc attached to it. The disc had red, yellow and green parts that were jumbled up. Vernu turned the disc to the right and a green part slid in to the outer circle. Stinu to the left and a red clicked next to it. Ali turned the wheel to the right and a yellow section clicked into place. Tina turned the disc and green bar fell into place, the chain it was attached to snatched it away. Ali turned the disc and a red bar was the wrong combination. Stinu turned it to yellow and it fitted.

"I wonder if this is the right grouping," Vernu said to no one in particular. She turned and green slotted in and then red. "It appears I was right. Everyone, try this for the next set: Red, yellow, green. They all took their turns and this was correct. The disc and the gate parted. They walked into the garden and found the red and yellow peppers easily.

Stinu dropped the monster hunter's coin pouch on the table in front of Tarquin. The mayor's eyes grew as wide as the sun.

"Here, use this to help rebuild the village," Stinu said.

"No you have been incredibly generous already, you keep it. We didn't expect to see it again, anyway."

"Well, seeing as you insist. I recommend you seal up the opening to the garden from the sewer. Leave a gap the size of a man. That will prevent any giant toads or other nasties getting down there."

"Consider it done!"

The villagers gathered in the square to wave

Them off and they made it back to the ship. Upon boarding The Sibell, the two women complained of stomach aches.

"I feel sick," Tina said and Vernu moaned.

And then they threw up.

"Page thirty five," Tina gasped before she passed out.

Stinu laid her on her bed and then he helped Ali put his mother to bed too. Stinu rushed to the lab and moved his finger over the bookshelf until he found what he was looking for.

It was a large maroon book with the words medicines, remedies and cures, embossed in gold leaf on the spine. Hurriedly, he placed the book on the table and leafed to page thirty five. His finger ran down the paragraphs until he found the words "Toad poison cure."

He barked out instructions to Ali who scooped up bottles and herbs and the two of them prepared the medicine. Two hours later and it was ready. They managed to tilt Tina's head and she drank the mixture, Vernu was still out cold.

"Lord, please enable mum to take her medicine," Ali prayed. Five minutes passed, and Vernu groaned. They managed to get her to take her cure too, and then the two men left them to get some rest.

Chapter Eighteen

Nadal untied the parchment from the leg of the carrier pigeon.

You must return to Tarnuz immediately! The King is making his own decisions again, which means somebody has not been giving him the mind control potion! I suspect that someone in the royal kitchen is also free of the drug. Your friend, Clepta.

After reading it, he screwed it up and threw it on the ground.

"Plot a course for Tarnuz. I have some urgent business to attend to," He growled at his captain and the ship began to turn.

***

"It was a gadget, it wasn't it," Ali said, as he watched the salty breeze blow through Tina's hair.

"That's rather cryptic. We've used a few on this trip. Which one are you referring to?" A week had past and, the two women had started to regain their strength. In a couple of days, they would be fit enough to disembark on the next island. They were in search of garlic.

"The Sarcosuchus. Both of you managed to subdue it very quickly. I think you used a Dyidian device to do it"

"Ah, that gadget. Yes you are correct. You fire a rope that hooks attached to it; a bit like a grappling hook, and the rope wraps around your victim and then the hooks embed themselves in to the ground. We had to fire at the same time. I took the head and your mother took the tail. You did the rest."

"You have to show me how to use one of those."

"Of course, but I hope we won't have to use them again. What kind of weird and wonderful beasts are coming up?"

Ali let out a big sigh. "Sadly, we are moving in to unknown territory. I can't tell you, because I don't know."

She could tell from the sad look on his face that he was telling the truth.

"I mean I could speculate, I suppose, but I don't think that would achieve anything."

"No, speculation is never a good idea, unless you are pretty certain of the outcome."

"We are all highly trained and prepared for anything. We also have had God on our side, too. We didn't have him at the start."

"You won't get an argument from me!"

They both smiled and watched the orange sun melt into the sea.

They cut their way through the bracken and they followed a path on the dales. They came ashore two hours ago and the terrain wasn't too bad, and although the sky threated rain, they hadn't felt any yet. The horses snorted but they didn't need to rest just yet. They rounded the hill then they came down the other side. They could see a village and the smoke from the cottage chimneys signalled life and beckoned them forwards. As they approached, the smell of burning spruce wafted towards them.

"I just hope they are friendly," Vernu said.

"Well, one thing is certain, they don't appear to be hiding, like the last people we met," Stinu said and the others nodded.

As they approached, some of the villagers eyed them suspiciously and mothers shooed their children into their houses. And then they were approached by a bald headed man with a neat ginger beard. He wore grey robes, with a white rope for a belt. He had a welcoming smile. He

"I don't trust this guy," Vernu said, leaning into Stinu's ear. Her gritted teeth made the phrase sound strange.

"Don't make a scene; I am sure we won't have too much to do with him," He replied, also through gritted teeth."

"Welcome, welcome. I am Norm, the village priest," He said, offering his hand to shake. Everyone shook his hand, but Vernu hesitated, and then she shook his hand.

Whilst they shook hands, Norm's smile looked strained, and he had a frightened look in his blue eyes. Vernu squeezed his hand a bit before she released her grip. Norm flexed his hand and then placed it in the pocket of his robes.

"Come this way, please," Norm said, and he led them to a modest house made from grey wood. They climbed the three steps on the porch and he opened the door. The house smelt of hops and various other plants and spices hung from the beams in the ceiling.

To the left was a kitchen with a white sink in the middle. After that, there was a door and then a short staircase, which probably led to the bedrooms. Next to that, there was a full bookcase, full of prayer books and a book called "How to listen." Next to the book case was a fire place and two pairs of socks hung over it, drying. At the back of the room was beer making equipment. The only light in the room came from the fire place. Norm busied himself lighting candles and lanterns that hung from the beams.

"Please, sit," He said and gestured to a kitchen table in the centre of the room with four wooden chairs.

There were no more chairs, so Norm had to stand. "

Would you like tea?" He said. They nodded. "Very good," He said and filled a large kettle with dried tea leaves and water and then he hung it from a hook on the fire place.

He added more wood and the temperature of the room increased. A short time later the kettle whistled. He retrieved the kettle and poured the tea into five cups on the kitchen table.

"Help yourselves," He said smiling at them but averted his eyes from Vernu.

Vernu watched him like a hawk, as she put the cup to her lips, her eyes brows raised as she drank the warm liquid. The tea was light and refreshing and tasted good. She looked in the cup and the tea was a light brown colour.

"How can I help you," Norm said.

"We are on a mission. We need ingredients for a meal we need to prepare to stop our country going to war with another larger country," Tina said.

"Yes, Tina is right. I am terribly sorry we haven't introduced ourselves. I am and Ali, this is my mother and royal chef, Vernu. This is Tina know it all and Dyidian expert. Tina poked her tongue out, but Ali waved it away with his hand a smile. And this is Stinu, sailor and warrior.

"I am very pleased to meet you. What ingredient brings you to Schguns "the quiet place?"

"Garlic, we are looking for garlic," Vernu said, boring her eyes into Norm. Norm looked at Ali for reassurance, and then he gulped. Producing a knife from somewhere, he started waving it around as if he needed confidence. The others scrapped their chairs back and drew their swords, four sharp tips pointing at the priest's neck and he gulped again.

"Oh, I am so sorry, I am not threatening anyone. It's just a thing I do when I tell a story.

"That's just as well, because we would cut you to shreds in seconds if you tried anything," Vernu snarled. "You are really trying my patience here, give me the knife and I promise you you'll get to live," She said, beckoning with her fingers. He leant forward and placed the knife in her palm, handle towards her. The others sat down, but now everyone had their eyes fixed on him.

"Tell us your story and make it quick. I am starting to get cross now. And make some more tea, while you're at it, too," Stinu said, pushing his teacup over the table. The others did the same.

"After you have finished your tea, I will take you to the finest wild garlic you could ever hope to find."

"Well, what are we waiting for," Tina said, draining her cup and standing up.

"Great, follow me." He led them around the back of the house. They walked past a wagon parked outside a stable. A brown horse neighed as he approached and he opened the stable door and fitted the horse to the wagon. They got in the back and he wagon pulled away.

Shortly after this, they started to feel drowsy. Vernu got up and drew her sword but her vision began to swim in front of her. The others got up too and they all fell on their backs on the floor of the wagon. Vernu could see a blurry face with a ginger beard peering at her and then she fell asleep.

Violent shaking of the wagon woke her.

Groaning, she looked at the others and they rubbed their eyes and then the wagon was flipped on its side. And they spilled on the ground. Still groggy, they got to their feet. They could see large ripples in the ground. It looked like a large mole or some other underground monster had caused the ripples.

It was a struggle to stand, but they held unto each other and helped each other to their feet. Slowly their vision cleared and another ripple came towards them, knocking them over, and Ali disappeared below ground.

The rippling stopped and a large worm burst from the earth with a loud roar, it opened its jaws, revealing rows and rows of teeth. It had another circular row of teeth just above its throat.

On its torso, it had hooks, three on the left and three on the right. The hooks looked like shark fins protruding through water but it used these for borrowing underground.

It reared its ugly head and spat venom at them, hitting Tina's shoulder armour. She yelped and jumped back and the armour sizzled and fizzed, but the metal covering protected her skin. Before she could retaliate, the worm had disappeared below ground again.

More wrinkles scarred the landscape and the worm surface again and Vernu had an idea. As the worm surfaced again, she waited for it to spray its acid, and then she darted behind it and rolled behind a hedge. Its venom caught its tail. The creature writhed and thrashed as its own acid burned its flesh.

There was more writhing from the worm. Its head thrashed about like an unattended garden hose with water running through it, spitting venom everywhere.

The adventurers ran away as the beast yielded to death and its neck crashed down and was still. Without hanging around, Vernu sprinted to the spot where Ali was last seen. There was a hole in wooden hatch that had been cut into the ground.

She lit her torch and looked in the hole, calling out his name.

"I am here, mum," Ali said, waving in her direction. Moving her flame, she could see the boy and he looked dirty, but unhurt.

"I am so glad you are alive. Are you hurt?"

"Apart from a few cuts and bruises I am fine."

"Can you climb up?" Stinu asked, waving his torch around the area.

"I think I could climb out if you dropped down a rope."

"I'll see if I can find a tree to tie the other end of the rope to," He said and went to look for a tree. After five minutes, the rope was lowered down and Ali began to climb to safety. As he was climbing, the rope went loose and he fell one and half metres to the floor. Before could say anything to the others, the ground shook and then heard cries from above, and the others clung to the slippery rocks and gradually make their way down to him.

"What happened up there?" Ali asked.

"We managed to defeat the Death Worm and then somebody cut the rope and threw rocks at us knocking into this hole, so here we are!" Tina said, dusting herself off.

"It's too slippery for us to get out, so we will have to carry on moving forward. I don't need you to tell me who cut the rope."

They all snorted.

"I don't think he was working alone. We were hit at the same time," Tina said.

"Yes. Norm and at least three other scumbags," Vernu said.

Tina moved towards Ali and began cleaning the cut above his left eye.

"Thanks. I can feel a draft coming from this direction," Ali said, pointing to the tunnel in front of them. "And seeing as it is the only way out, it looks like we have no choice but to follow it."

They all nodded and started walking down the tunnel. The black rocks were propped up by wooden beams and they saw grooves cut into the stones. It was an old coal mine.

After a short walk down the tunnel, they came to a room on the left. It contained various iron swords and shields. Each person picked one sword and shield and fastened them to their left hips.

They walked for another hour before they saw daylight and they pulled themselves out into the bright sun. They covered their eyes as they adjusted to the daylight. When they refocused, they saw a beautiful meadow. The floor was carpeted with wild flowers and the air was filled with a lovely floral aroma.

Bees buzzed from flower to flower and they saw cows chewing the cud.

To the left of them were a stream and a row of trees. They walked to the stream and Vernu made a fire. The rest of them fished, and they ate what they caught with crusty bread.

When they had finished their meal, they saw a horse and cart coming towards them. The driver wore a wide brimmed straw hat and sandy coloured clothes. When he got close, they flagged him down and he came to a stop.

"Afternoon. I don't think I's seen you here's before," The man said with a famer's accent.

"I wonder if you could help us. We have been double-crossed by a bald priest. Average height and has a neat ginger beard. What can you tell us about him?"

"Aye, that would be that Norm you be squawking about. He be as slippery as an eel and as cunning as a forx," He said, scratching his grey side burns his right hand and switching the straw stalk from one side of his mouth to the other. "Did he make yous sleep?"

"Yes, he put something in our tea!" Vernu said, gripping the hilt of her sword, subconsciously.

"Aye, that is a classic trick of his. He only does that to people when wants. He's a coward, see."

"You seem to know an awful lot about him. Why haven't you done anything to stop him yourself?" Tina asked.

"I don'ts have anything to do with him. He stays out of my way and I stays out of his," He said, scratching his sun burnt bulbous nose. "He needs to be stopped. He has tricked a lot of folks. If you don't mind, I need to see to my ladies," He said, pointing that the Jersey cows in the meadow.

"Thank you," Stinu said, stepping aside and letting the farmer pass.

"Let me know how you get on," The farmer said without turning his head.

"Will do," Stinu said, and then to himself: "Fat lot of good he was!"

"I think we should all press on," Vernu said, and the others agreed.

The road became a gentle slope, and then it became a mountain path. Goats bleated as they passed them on the opposite side of the path.

By the time the sun had started its descent, they had walked the perimeter of the mountain and the path slanted downwards.

Tina stopped and wiped her brow. Looking up, she saw birds of prey circling in the air, heads down, getting ready to swoop down and catch a bite to eat.

She thought about Zilli and wondered how he was doing. She knew he was in expert hands and Galaxio would take care of him, but she missed them both.

One of the birds of prey dived and carried away a small rodent, maybe a rat or a weasel, and she sighed to herself.

I can't wait for this all to be over, but there is still a fair bit of the mission left yet. She thought.

When they were on flat ground, they came to another meadow and they saw deer. Some nibbled leaves from trees others nibbled the grass and some ate from bushes. The gang got close, and they were surprised to see that the deer let them stroke them.

"As lovely as these animals are, we really should push on. We don't know what Norm has planned for us," Tina said.

"Bye, Deano," Ali said, waving at a young stag.

They carried on their journey and as they did so, the terrain became more and more sparse. Eventually, they came to a desert. An angry sand storm raged and a women's scream could be heard from within. The heroes drew their swords.

Chapter Nineteen

Nadal strode across the jetty, almost knocking Clepta flying.

"Nadal, you need to calm down. We can get a handle on this!"

"Really," Nadal said stopping, nostrils flaring and eyes burning. "If you had a handle on it already, I wouldn't need to come here. Do. Your. Job. Properly!" He said jabbing his finger in the little man's chest as he spoke.

"I have had a lot on my mind. Bea has left me." He said, trying not to cry.

"I can't understand what has happened."

"I can. It's called incompetence and I intend to fix it. Perhaps you should think less about your marriage and more about the task at hand!" He said, striding ahead, his robes flowing behind him. "Arrange a card game," He said, without turning around.

Mosquitos buzzed around them as Clepta dealt the cards. It would have been better to close the wooden blinds, but the heat was intense and the tiny upper room had a heavy smoky atmosphere. Waitresses poured drinks in between cigar puffs and male laughter. Gradually, the room tipped in

Nadal's favour and every cook, kitchen porter and royal servants were under his command.

"Excellent, he said, rubbing his hands together, with a gleam in his eyes. "I knew a strong potion would do the trick!"

"Have you tested this one, master? Do you know if there are any side effects?"

"Side effects?" He roared, standing up in disgust. "I am dealing with the side effects of the weaker drug right now!" "How did you ever expect us to conduct our business with the king watching every move I make?" "It will only take a day or two and Tarnuz will be under my control again," He said picking up a large orange and crushing it in his hand, the juices dripping through his fingers and down his wrist.

Two days of freedom ended when Nadal regained control of Tarnuz. When he was satisfied with the results, Nadal boarded his ship and plotted to intercept The Sibell.

***

The sand storm turned fierce and so did the screaming Banshee. Before their ears bled, the four of them placed bees wax in their ears. The Banshee circled them, bringing the sand cloud with her and mouthed things they couldn't hear, something about their deaths.

Remembering the iron sword he had picked up from the coal mine, Ali drew it and the Banshee screamed louder and her eyes flashed red.

The storm grew stronger and they battled to stay on their feet. The Banshee sped towards Stinu, who swung, slicing the Banshee's right shoulder.

The monster screamed, but the storm lessened. Tina swung slicing its torso and then Vernu hacked its left leg. Ali lunged, driving his sword into the creature's heart and watched as the red light in her eyes went out and the stormed died with her.

Chests heaved in and out as they stared at each other. They looked like four sparrows after an enthusiastic dust bath.

"They travel on their own don't they, these Banshee things?" Vernu said to her son.

"Thankfully, they do," he said, and then he yawned.

"I was hoping you would say that," she said, wiping dust from her brow.

"I hate to be the bringer of bad news, but do we actually know how to find the garlic?" Tina said.

"Yes, now that we know Norm can't be trusted," Stinu added.

"Look, on the horizon. The terrain changes to more mountains over there. If we can find a cave, I will show you the place we will find garlic."

They agreed to head toward the mountains and at sunset; they reached a cave and Ali laid out his map on the dusty floor, which he pinned down with a stone in each corner. They had extra light from the torch holders in the cave wall, a welcome relic from a bygone age.

"According to the map, we are right slap dab in the middle of garlic country. If we head a mile or so down river, we should find garlic."

"Then back to the village for a showdown with Norm," Vernu said, whilst sharpening her sword.

"Vernu, what's for dinner?" Tina said.

"Pan fried pork with onions and potatoes and an apple sauce."

"Yummy!" Tina said.

"Do you know what annoys the most about this trip? We have most of these ingredients back home."

"I get that. But then again, we have never had to work this closely before, and yet we all work for King Stefano. "We have all seen each other in passing, but we have really developed a close bond. We have had lots of wonderful adventures and have cheated death many times. But, I don't think I am alone in this, we have discovered parts of a miracle book, and that is by far the most exciting part of my adventure." Stinu said, as he poked the fire with a stick. Everyone agreed.

"We are like a family. Well, we are parts of two different families, and, like any family, we don't always see eye to eye, but we all know that we are stronger together," Tina said.

"That is undeniable. I may go off on one every now and again, but I do really appreciate you all. I hope we have many more adventures, but I have a feeling this amazing book is going to take us in many different directions."

"I'll drink to that," Stinu said raising his wooden flagon of apple juice and they all knocked them together.

"Let's get some sleep. Goodnight everyone," Vernu said.

"Goodnight," They all said.

Ali turned on his side away from them, with a smile on his face.

In the morning, they had scrambled eggs, Ali's favourite and after that, they travelled to the garlic. When they had gathered up everything they needed, a strange and scary looking creature galloped up to them and they all drew their swords. It had the body of a horse and a single antler in the centre its head.

"Don't be alarmed by frightening appearance. I come in peace. My name is Xiezhi. I am a guardian of truth and justice," Xiezhi said, in a deep male voice that helped the gang relax. "I help you. I have heard that a man named Norm has caused you harm."

"Yes, that is true," Vernu said, tightening her grip on her sword.

"I mean you no harm. You can trust me. Climb on my back and I will take you to the village. I make sure you and the villagers get justice for all the bad things he has done. Please climb on my back," And he lowered himself to the ground and they climbed on to his back and gripped onto his black mane and he began to gallop back the village.

"Am I going too fast?"

"Actually, could you move a bit faster, please?" Tina said.

Xiezhi picked up his speed and trees, hills, mountains, streams and deserts whizzed past as the adventurers held on for life. It wasn't long, and they saw familiar buildings and plumes of smoke from the village.

As Xiezhi came to a stop, Vernu dismounted first and marched up three steps and knocked on Norm's door. He opened the door and when he saw Vernu; he fled to the toilet.

Before he opened the door, Vernu threw a knife pinning him to the door by his armpit sleeve. Eyes wide with fright, he tried to pull himself free, but Vernu threw another which pinned the bottom left of his robe. Then another knife pinned his right armpit sleeve and then one final knife pinned the bottom of his robe. She aimed to throw again, but having no intention of throwing it.

"Please, don't hurt me. What I did was wrong," he said and sobbed.

"I just did it to prove a point. You nearly got us all killed, more than once too. Anyway, it's out of my hands. We have someone we'd like you to meet. He is a guardian of justice and he will put a stop to all the little schemes you've got going on," She said, and began retrieving her knives from the door.

"Whatever you say. I have heard that Xiezhi is fair and honourable," He said rubbing his wrists and quivering.

"We know you weren't working alone, so I suggest you make sure your accomplices stand trial, too."

"The-they are hiding in the- the stables. They heard that the townsfolk wanted to beat them."

"I wonder why? Let's not keep Xiezhi waiting."

When they opened the door, they could see that a crowd had gathered and Xiezhi stood in the middle. It was hard to tell if he was happy or sad as his face seemed to have a permanent scowl.

"He has at least three men helping him. They are hiding in his stable," Vernu shouted and six men went to the stable and brought three men before Xiezhi.

"What are your names?" Xiezhi said, as he walked passed the line of men, scrutinising their faces.

The on nearest to Norm said he was called Henry, next to him was Arthur and the last was known as Edward.

"These here men have caused many problems to me ladies. Some been slaughtered before theirs times," The farmer said from the crowd. The straw from his mouth had gone but the hat was still in place. "If they had shared the profits from their sales, I would have turned a blind eye, so I would," He added.

"I caught that one there," An angry man said, pointing at Henry. "Stealing one of my hens. He soon dropped it when my hay fork pinched his bum!" The villagers laughed loudly.

"Silence," Xiezhi boomed. "These are serious matters. I need to hear all of the evidence so I can decide what kind of punishment to give this gang of bandits." He listened as villager after villager told stores of theft and some falling asleep and finding themselves in dangerous situations, and then the adventurers told their story.

"I can see that the only thing that would help these criminals to right the wrong they have done by spending time in the village prison; unless there is something you could give back to the village. Norm, what do you have to offer?"

"W-well, I, I h-have a lovely beer," he said.

"Bring me a flagon of this beer and let me try for myself," Xiezhi said. "You, you and you," He said pointing his antler at three village guards. "Accompany Norm to his house and make sure he doesn't try any tricks."

"Yes sir!" They said and frog marched Norm to his house. Two minutes later they emerged carrying a flagon full of beer. One of the guards held it to Xiezhi's lips and he gulped it down noisily. He gasped and smacked his lips.

"Delicious. I propose that you make this beer for the villagers, under close scrutiny of the guards for free, until you have put right the harm you have done. After this period and when the village is completely satisfied, you will be allowed to sell your beer legitimately at a reasonable rate. If I find out that your business is operating illegally, then you will be thrown into jail immediately. Do you understand the terms of your punishment?"

"Yes we do, thank you so much, oh just one," The bandits said.

"You must apologise to the garlic hunters and as a way of saying sorry, you must send ten percent of all beer made to Tarnuz."

"Yes we will, go great one."

"Very good, don't let me down," And then he turned to the four heroes "My sincerest of apologies to you all. May you go in peace."

"Thank you," They said and mounted their horses and rode back to The Sibell.

All four of them watched the sun sink into the sea from the stern.

"Have we just survived the strangest mission yet?" Ali said, drinking apple juice from his flagon.

"I think that is fair to say, yes," Tina said and the other two agreed.

"You really had it in for Norm, didn't you, Vernu. Thank goodness for Xiezhi. If it wasn't for him, I think you would have taken Norm's head off!" Stinu said.

"I don't think it would have come to that, but I am pleased to see justice was served. Also, Tarnuz gets to benefit from it, too. I am looking forward to serving beer to The King and cooking a steak and ale pie, too."

"Ah, Tarnuz. How I miss you," Stinu said as the sunset on another day.

Chapter Twenty

It was an unpleasant job, but somebody had to do it and it was Ali's turn.

He shovelled the steaming horse manure in to a bucket and carried it to Vernu's vegetable patch and spread it on the plants. *How could something so smelly be so valuable?* He thought. He wanted to hold his nose, but the job prevented him from doing so.

Finally, his job was done, and he got up and stretched his back, then he bent down and replaced the shovel and the bucket.

As he returned to his room, and the maid curtsied, stepping away from the steaming bath that she had prepared.

When he was alone, he stripped and got into the water. It was just right.

Tina had made a new soap, so he took it from the side of the bath and sniffed. It smelt of strawberries and was as red as them, too. He lathed up, and the soap made him feel hungry.

He would get a bowl of strawberries after his bath.

The clean bath towel was in reach and he pulled it off the towel rail. After drying himself, he put on clean clothes and boots.

Then he went and asked his mum for two bowls of strawberries; one for him and one for Tina. When he entered the lab, Tina had her back to him and she was writing labels and placing them on more strawberry soap bars.

"Here, I bought you this," He said, handing her a bowl of strawberries. "That's as if you haven't had enough of strawberries by now, of course."

She took the bowl and smiled at him.

"Thanks. No, I love them. The process for making soap is very different, anyway."

"How is it different?"

"Well, there aren't much strawberries used. I use cooking oil, vitamin E liquid, and strawberry pulp. Then I use goat soap mixture and there you have it!" She said, eyes glowing as she dug into her fruit. "They were yummy," She said, rubbing her tummy.

"Sounds simple when you describe it like that. Apart from making salty sailors smell nice, what other use do you have for them?"

"Hadn't you thought about the markets in Tarnuz?"

"No, I hadn't thought about them at all. Should I think about them?"

"Yes. Once we have served the royal meal to The King, people will be keen to serve the dish to their families at home. We will need to sell some ingredients in the market so they can do that." "I thought the soap would be a little side-line."

"Ah, I see that makes sense. What do you think I should sell?"

"Well, why don't you ask your mother? What do you think of the soap?"

"I thought was very nice," He said and sniffed his wrist it had a faint scent of strawberries. "I don't think it's a very masculine smell, though. Do you think you could make something that is more, err, manly?"

She laughed. "Of course. I think there would be a few grumbling sailors if I gave them all strawberry soap!"

"I won't argue with you there! I'll see mum again and ask her what she thinks I should sell at the markets."

"Okay and I'll start work on "soap for men," Bringing her fists together across her torso.

He laughed. "See you later."

"See you then."

His mother was talking to one chef they were preparing a white fish dish with wild rice for lunch.

"Hello son," She said. "Have you come back for more strawberries?" "Lunch won't be long, so I wouldn't eat anymore, if I were you."

"No, I am fine. I wanted to ask you a question."

"Okay, go ahead."

"What do you think I should sell at the Tarnuz market, when we get back?"

She had finished washing the fish scales from her hands and was drying them on a towel.

"That's a good question. Did Tina tell you about the market?"

He nodded.

"Well, I have been buying from the markets for years and I think I take for granted the bright and colourful stories the traders tell me. I am sure that I bought more from the sellers with the best stories! I don't know if they did that deliberately or not. Select the story that you could tell the best and decide which product that it relates to."

"I see what you are saying. I am not sure if it is an adventure we have already had or one we haven't had yet.

"You don't have to decide until our quest is over, but my advice would be to tell a story that gives people hope. I wouldn't tell the story of how Nadal captured, for example. You don't want to scare your customers away!"

"That's very true, but it also depends on how you tell the story. I doubt I will tell people about the spider fight, either. Tina and Stinu didn't do very well there and people fear spiders enough already, without me adding to their fear."

"That's very smart thinking. A good leader inspires people and gives them someone to admire and look up to. Especially young children."

"Thanks mum, that was very helpful."

"You're welcome. I think we will do a brilliant trade when we return."

"I think you're right. I am going to find Stinu and see what he thinks." He found Stinu piloting the ship. He was whistling a tune he didn't know, probably a sea shanty.

"Hi Stinu! Why do you still pilot the ship when you have an entire crew to do it for you?"

"That's simple. We are a man down; Galaxio is still caring for Zilli. Also, this is one of those calm sea days, beautiful time to enjoy sailing. Also, I enjoy it."

"That's fair enough. I have been talking about the Tarnuz market with mum and Tina. What does it mean to you?"

"Well, although the king pays us very well, sometimes it necessary to sell some rare treasures to finance something. If you come across a shrewd bandit trying to charge you more than an item's worth, you may need to pay extra. I would rather pay more and stay alive!"

"Yes, I value life more than I do riches. What do you plan to sell at the market?"

"I am not sure yet. I might take the easy option and just help Tina sell her stuff. The best sellers are the ones with the most interesting stories."

"That's funny, mum said the same thing!"

"It's true, though! Think about some sellers you have bought from in the past."

"I went to this seller one I was a kid. I loved pink coconut ices. I picked out the ones I wanted and the seller just wrapped them in brown parchment, snatched the money from my hand and thrust my sweets at me. I ran back to my mother crying. Mother took me back there and made the mean old man apologise. We found another sweet seller who was kind, smiley and told marvellous stories. He even used to give me extra sweets from time to time." "I can see your point."

"There you are. I think when we get back to Tarnuz, you will have so many stories to tell, and you won't know where to start!"

"That sounds like a pleasant problem to have!"

"Maybe, just don't lose any sleep over it!" He said, and then he rang the bell above his head. "Land ahoy!" He yelled and the rest of the crew sprang it action. They had reached their destination, an island called Scheaf. (To dwell).

Chapter Twenty One

It was a two-day journey to the other side of the island. They were going to meet a man called Mercado; he would sell them the smoked paprika they needed.

"Maybe this island will give us some treasure we could sell or trade at the market," Stinu said.

"I guess we will have to wait and see," Vernu said.

"The greatest treasure for me would find more of the old book," Tina said.

No one answered as they pondered on what she said. Ali let the sound of the horses' hooves and the snorts from the animals soothed him. As they continued, they approached a walled city. Two guards with curved helmets and red tunics crossed their pikes, preventing them from entering the city.

"State your business," One said.

Stinu dismounted and walked towards them.

"We are travelling to the other side of the island. We are to meet a man called Mercado. He is going to sell us smoked paprika."

"Let them in, let them!" A voice said from behind the portcullis. They could see a short blond headed popping about. "I am Armand and I am the baron's chief of staff. I think the baron would be interested in hiring to deal with a slight problem we have been having. Would you be prepared to help us?"

"Have we got monster hunters stamped on our foreheads, or what?" Ali said, to Stinu out the side of his mouth.

"We kind of fall into that category, I am afraid. Yes I think we can help you," He said to Armand.

"Splendid. Raise the gate!" And slowly the portcullis disappeared, and the travellers got back on their horses and rode through the entrance. The gate lowered when they were inside.

"What seems to be the problem?"

"We have a bit of a situation with a monster, I am afraid. Well, not a monster more of man behaving like a monster, but I'll let the baron explain it all to you." They passed market sellers offering everything from fresh fish to new boots. Herbalists sold exotic potions. And the market square was filled with jugglers, acrobats and children playing street games. Horses pulled carts and carriages and the air was full of smells of food, perfume and horse manure. Somewhere a blacksmith was hammering steel. They followed Armand up a stone slope and they stopped at a stone building with a heavy oak door. It had an enormous fist for a door knocker, and Armand rapped it three times.

"It's Armand. I have the guests for the baron."

There was a pause, followed by deadbolts sliding and keys jangling, then the door opened a crack. A man's beady eye appeared at the door and it rolled around, taking in the adventurers.

"Come in," He said with a creepy voice, swinging back the door. He was a short bald man with grey tufts of hair on each side of his head. He had a curved spin and leaned on his walking sticking. He peered over his glasses at them and his lips puckered up as he studied them. Then he reached into his dirty red waist coat and squinted at his gold pocket watch, replacing and with a wave of his hand, he said.

"This way please," gesturing to an enormous staircase covered with red carpet.

As they climbed the stairs, Ali gazed around him. The room had dark panelling, and it was decorated with suits of armour, pictures of men slaying legendary beasts and family portraits. As they climbed higher, they faced a portrait of a portly man with a dark beard flecked with grey.

He wore red robes with gold trimmings on the sleeves and hems. He had a kind expression, but there was sadness in his eyes. The plaque at the bottom read: "Baron Ivan John Borthwick II"

Upon reaching the top, they turned right at the portrait and the old man knocked on another dark wooden door.

"Yes?" I deep voice bellowed from behind the door.

"Lord Baron, it is Horace. I have the guests for you."

"Well, don't dilly dally man, send them in!"

"Yes, right away. You may enter," He said and showed them into the room. The room was decorated with lighter wood panels, more portraits and family a family painting with a younger slimmer baron and attractive red-haired lady and a pretty red-haired girl; the baron's wife and daughter. But this was the only evidence of them in the room. The picture hung above the fireplace, but the fire wasn't enough to light the room. Heavy red drapes, matching the baron's clothes; hung from the windows. The drapes were drawn even though it was mid-day.

"Welcome to Scheaf or the little corner of it I control," He said, smiling, but eyes his were dead. "Would you like anything to drink?" He said pouring more red wine into the golden goblet in his hand.

"Could we have some coffee, please?" Stinu said.

"Horace, could you make our guests coffee, please?"

"Yes sir, right away sir," he said, and the butler disappeared to make coffee.

"What brings you to these parts?"

"Long story short, we need ingredients. We have a meeting with Mercado. He is going to sell us some smoked paprika," Vernu said.

"Mercado is a good man, and he is well versed in herbs and spices, but if its paprika you want, I have plenty. There's something you're not telling me," he said, and then he drank from his goblet.

Horace returned with a silver tray. It had five china cups, a coffee urn, cream, sugar and some cake slices decorated with flaked almonds on them. The aroma of coffee and almonds, made Ali's mouth water. "Please sit and enjoy. Then you can tell me all about your quest. You all look like you have many stories to tell," he persisted. Taking their seats, Ali grabbed an almond slice and took a large bite. It was sweet with jam in the middle. He closed his eyes and savoured the rest of the dessert, and then he poured coffee, added cream and three sugars. Tina raised her eyebrows at him.

"What? I'm hungry."

"Yes, but ever happened to ladies first," She said and reached across him and served herself; Cake, coffee, cream, but no sugar. Stinu had the same as her, Vernu just had coffee and cream, and then she told the baron everything. All about King Khalid and Nadal's mind control potions. He listened intently, fingers in a pyramid. Nodding when he needed to and laughing when it amused him and turning serious again when Vernu had finished her story.

The baron reflected for a while, and the only sound came from the fire as it crackled and popped.

"You have been very honest with me and will be honest with you.

I was twenty when I met my beloved Charlotte," He walked over to the fireplace and was looking at the family picture.

"My parents had a bride picked out for me when I was sixteen, but I had no interest in her and she had none in me.

Both of us had to present our cases to our families and wasn't easy, but we stayed friends.

A short while after this, I went travelling, see a bit of the world and stand on my own two feet.

My mother was putting pressure on me every day, and I was tired of the endless stream of pretty maidens she paraded in front of me.

They were fine, but they didn't seem to have any spirit.

I made a promise to stay close to the castle to begin with, and mother was pleased.

It suited me to be nearby, and I trained with tracker who was a weapons expert. I stayed with him for two years, one year longer than I intended to.

When I turned eighteen, my parents couldn't stop me I said my tearful goodbyes and sailed the seas.

I visited exotic landscapes, braved wind, rain, snow and sand and probably visited places you have too.

Two years after this, I heard about the tournament in Tanur (the place where the water flows together) and entered. Men and women could enter and it combined horse riding, archery, marathons, swimming, and sword fighting. This fiery redhead, who won the tournament, impressed me. I came a close second and at the tournament winner's feast; we shared a beer together and then eventually she became my wife. We married in the spring and my dear sweet Elizabeth was born the following year that was sixteen years ago. Today is Elizabeth's sixteenth birthday."

"Do you mind if I ask what happened to them?" Tina said, with a compassionate tone.

The baron gave a heavy sigh before he continued.

"I have you heard the legend of Count Serrat?"

"Isn't that the one who is condemned to ride a horse with hell hounds running after him?" Tina said.

"That's the one. It's not a legend, it is true. He controls a goldmine in the hills. The mine is run by a band of goblins. He captures people and forces them to work there as his slaves. My girls went out during the day and must have got lost. And they never came home. That was two years ago."

"Why didn't you rescue them?" Stinu said.

"We tried, but the Count and his goblins are cunning and I lost men. I wanted to keep trying and never give up, but the townsfolk threatened to hang me if anymore loved ones died to save mine."

"What makes you think we would succeed when so many others have failed," Ali said, after he had eaten all the cakes.

"I have been praying The Lord has said that he would send warriors to help me in my time of need and they would deliver me from my enemies."

No one spoke, and then Stinu broke the silence.

"Okay, we will help you. What can you tell us about the Count? Does he have weaknesses we can exploit?"

"As part of his punishment, he is permanently on fire. If we could bombard him with water, we should be able to rid the island of him once and for all. If we could kill his hell hounds, he would weaken and we should have an advantage."

"I have an idea. I will need to speak to your armourer," Tina said.

"I can arrange that."

"Is there any way you can convince the rest of the town to take one last stand against evil?" Ali said.

"I am not sure I can say anything to change their minds. I think they stopped listening to me a long time ago."

"May be I will convince them," Stinu said.

"I need all the help I can get. I am certain that folk have loved ones trapped in those mines, but are to scare or too proud to admit it."

"Right, I am going to stand in the town square and see if we can gather an army. When are you most likely to see the Count?"

"He is nocturnal, but he doesn't normally appear until 10p.m."

"Right, I think we should pray."

And they all bowed their heads.

"Vernu, do you want to lead us?"

"Yes of course. Lord, I pray you will help the baron have courage. I pray the townsfolk will get behind the baron and will fight to free their loved ones. Give us the wisdom to defeat our enemies and may the blacksmith help Tina. Amen."

"Amen." They all said.

They all made their way to the square and the baron's bell got everyone's attention.

"Hear ye, hear ye. May I present to you today Cilistinu of Tarnuz?"

Stinu walked onto the stage, and all eyes fastened on him.

"Life can be a struggle, and I know it's difficult to stand up to evil. My friends and I come from Tarnuz, and our way of life is being threatened by a king from a larger country. We need to succeed, because we know it will bring peace to our nation. If we stand together today, you can see peace you land, too. We have been sent here by God and in his victory we trust."

The crowd roared, and some threw their hats in the air.

Rain and hail pelted the ground, and Stinu hoped the Count would still show. Ten minutes later and the faint sound of horse's hooves and baying hounds got closer.

The Count came to the target area and the battle catapult fired its hitting mark. The Count's horse reared and its flames smouldered. It would be awhile before the water bombs could be re-loaded.

The foot soldiers charged at the hell hounds. Some fired water bombs from hand held catapults, others slashed at the creatures. Many fell, but the remaining pack circled and charged again. The Count's horse recovered and charged, but the battle catapult spoke again and the count was no more. The battle raged for fifteen minutes, and then the hounds were defeated.

The army moved to the mine, and the army released their dogs and horses in the mine. Five minutes passed and goblins ran out of the mine screaming. Some fell to the ground, writhed around on the floor. The army spent fifteen minutes battling the fiends, and the goblins were no more. They reunited people with their families. When everyone was clear of the mine, Tina's team blew it up, closing it forever.

The baron hugged his family, and although they were dirty and thin, they were unharmed. Everyone returned home and the following day the baron threw a feast for everyone. The crew sat a table further from the celebrations for a quick exit. The baron found them and shook all of their hands with enthusiasm.

"I can't thank you enough. Please expect this as a token of my appreciation," He said stepping aside and Horace pushed a wooden wheelbarrow loaded with money sacks.

"We couldn't possibly take all this," Stinu said.

"No, you must take it. It is a small price to pay for bringing my family back together."

"Stinu, take the money," Ali said out of the side of his mouth.

"We will gladly accept. We will need to send a message to our crew and then they can take this gift back to the ship. When they arrive, we will need to leave."

"That is absolutely fine."

Vernu released a crow, and then the crew arrived two hours later.

"It time for us to go," Stinu said.

"Bring it in, let's have a group hug," The baron said, and they hugged and said their goodbyes.

Chapter Twenty Two

Unrelenting, the sun beat down on them even though it was half-past two. The horses panted, and they sweated as much as the humans.

The orchard provided some shade; the ground was still hot on the horse's feet. The group pulled on to the grass area so save the horses' more pain. They carried on through the tall yellow grass and they came to an oasis. They dismounted and the horses drunk from the water. To cool down, the gang swam in the water, then they got the horses and they swam too. When the sun sunk a little lower in the sky, the team carried on. They journeyed for another two hours and it was starting to get dark. They came to an abandoned mansion, and they decided they would camp there for the night. The door had a puzzle on the front of it. It had two discs with symbols that had to be matched up. They were bird, cat, dog, and mouse. Ali went first, matching dog, cat, bird, and mouse and as the two discs moved the door opened.

"Beginner's luck," Tina said nudging him in the ribs and barging passed him.

"Well, it opened, didn't it, beginner's luck or not!"

"Don't let her get to you, son."

"Well done, Ali," Stinu said.

A chill wind whistled through the glassless windows, and the dirty shredded curtains flapped in the breeze, warning the house that there were intruders. Crystal candelabras hung from the ceiling, and to their right was a marble staircase. It was as white as tombstones. Floorboards creaked above them, and trees stretched their skeletal fingers through the window frames. Tree roots had lifted off the tiled flooring as if nature resented the mansion.

"Do we sleep here or on the first floor?" Stinu offered.

"Let's find the most secure place first," Tina said.

They moved to the right and found another door and opened on to a study. It had no windows, but it had a fireplace. There was a hole in the ceiling, but it looked cosy enough.

"This will do," Tina said

Ali found some wood and on the third attempt, the fire lit.

Vernu made ham salad baguettes, and they had apples for dessert. After this, they went to sleep.

In the morning, Vernu boiled eggs on the fire and then they departed.

They had to wade through a large puddle to get to their horses, but the stables had kept the animals safe and dry. They travelled the complete day and by nightfall; they reached Mercado's town. Faces appeared at windows, but when they saw the group their shutters closed, and suspicious eyes looked out with caution. Frightened glances drove people to their homes, and deadbolts sealed them in.

"Something has got this town spooked," Tina said.

"Yes. I am hoping Mercado can enlighten us," Vernu said.

Lit torches led them to the trader's house. It was a converted barn with a staircase on the right, leading to a door with a large round window above it. The window frame was cross shape and a yellow glow welcomed them in, a beacon of hope for a town living in fear. When they climbed the stairs, Stinu knocked on the door.

A spy hole opened in the door and brown eye darted back and forth analysing the group.

"Names."

The eye said. Stinu cleared his throat.

"I am Admiral Cilistinu of the Tarnuz Royal Navy; we have Valentina, my daughter, Vernu and her son Alessandro."

"Just a minute," the voice said, and the spy hole slid shut and the door was opened.

When the door opened, they faced a tall, broad middle-aged man, who had a large brown beard, unkempt hair and crow's feet at the corner of his humourless eyes,

"Welcome to my spice emporium," he said, waving to the spice racks. His tone was sad and tired, and he had no joy in his step. This floor was labelled N-Z. He moved his finger across the racks until he found the letter P and then he produced a five kilo bag of smoked paprika and handed it to Vernu. He slumped into an armchair and gulped down something from a tin flagon. He gasped and wiped his beard. "If you need more, send word and I'll have some shipped out to you."

"Something very strange is going on here," Ali said "There are people living in fear and you seem very unhappy. Could you tell us what has happened, we will be able to help."

Mercado sighed, massaged his temples, and leaned forward.

"Cuegle is what happened. It has been taking children away. People won't venture out after dark, and traders refuse to come here. It's terrible for business. If something isn't done, I will run out of supplies and it will force me to close."

"I think the children of the town are more important than your business," Vernu said, fixing her gaze on him.

"I am sorry. I don't have any children and my wife died, so the business is all I have."

Vernu continued to stare at him, pondering his words. His demeanour didn't change.

"I believe you. It seems we have a second job: dealing with unwanted attention from beasts! Where was the last sighting of this Cuegle?"

"I'll take you there," he said, standing up. They went out the door they came in and he locked the door behind him. Vernu left the paprika behind.

They walked for half an hour and they came to clearing. There was a huge thatched cottage, and a tree grew next to it. A cage hung from one branch, and sobs and moans could be heard. It was the village children. The children were stick thin and had dirty faces. Some had bald patches on their scalps.

Tina looked away and choked back tears. Then, huge grotesque creature came out of the cottage. It had one horn in the centre of its forehead and its three eyes blinked as it prodded the cage with a large branch. The cage swung backwards and forwards and some children yelled, some screamed, and others cried. The beast laughed like a clap of thunder. Ali whistled.

"Over here, handsome!"

The beast stopped smiling and faced the unknown voice. The fiend had three arms without fingers and ran towards snapping its pincers. It attacked, but Ali rolled away and the creature planted its arms in the ground.

It snarled and lashed out at Ali again; the others joined the fight. It gained speed, and they stepped out of the way, but it knocked Stinu to the ground and then Mercado too.

The others fired arrows and slashed with swords, and Tina stood in front of a large holly bush. She chopped at the creature's legs with her hatchet and it dived at her, and she tripped on the holly and fell over. The Cuegle tried to free itself, but it was too late. It screamed as the holly burned its flesh. A minute passed and the air smelt of burnt flesh and burnt holly and the monster was gone. The gang rescued the children and escorted them back to the village.

Drums banged, flutes and lyres, and other instruments played, and people danced. The celebrations were quickly assembled, but the sun shone on a new day and the children were safe. The party went on until sunset and the crew said goodbye to the village and they were thrilled that they brought their children home.

"I have sent word that it is safe to trade with our village again. I should be able to get my business up and running again by the end of the week, thanks to you."

"You're welcome," Stinu said.

Somebody tapped Mercado on the shoulder and he turned around and a pretty blond lady with plaits smiled at him.

"Would you like to dance with me, Mercado?"

"Ah, Ingrid, I would love to," The smile had returned to his face and eyes and he wave as the lady tugged him towards the festivities.

"Right, shall we make our way back to The Sibell, then?" Tina said.

They nodded and made the two-day journey back to the ship.

Chapter Twenty Three

With one eye open, Ali watched the seagull circle their heads and leave. He breathed out a sigh, grateful that the bird hadn't pooed on him. It was another warm day and the sea breeze blew gently on his face.

"I bet you thought you were a goner when you tripped yesterday," he said, moving his dead leg back in to the hammock and rubbing his foot.

"That's a pretty daft question. You can't think about it when you're unconscious, can you? I am glad we reunited those kids with their families, though," she said, shielding her eyes with her hat and rocking her hammock from side to side.

"I am just showing concern. How do you feel about helping people with their monster problems?"

"Thank you for your concern. The more we do, the greater the risk. We have more chance of being injured or even killed, but we can't ignore the cry for help. None of us are motivated by greed or power. We have a desire to do the right thing."

"Agreed. Some of them reward us, and I know we aren't in it for the money, but your dad had a point about needing to barter with traders from time to time."

"I am surprised we haven't had to help people sooner if I'm honest."

"I think that is purely because we have travelled to uninhabited islands. There was evidence of the Dyidians on some of them, maybe that's why."

"I am looking forward to finding more Dyidian artefacts," She said, rubbing her hands.

A shadow blocked out the sun.

"Sorry to disturb your downtime, but we are about to dock," Stinu said.

"Okay, let's see what we will face on the island of Tschareins," springing in to action, Ali drew his sword.

Stinu and Tina rolled their eyes.

"What? It's important to be ready at all times!"

"Come on eager beaver, let's go!"

The island's shoreline was dotted with cottages and villas with terracotta roofs. Every now and again, there was a shrine to someone. As they their horses travelled further, the shrines became more frequent. There was a bigger problem here.

I am wondering if there are any heroes left on this island. Stinu thought. The road sloped round to the right, and they saw a temple. It had two spires, and each one had a gold dome on top. The bell tolled and Stinu hoped it was for morning prayers and not another funeral. There was an eerie quietness in the air, but the air buzzed with bees and the scent of crocus and other flowers. Life was determined to carry on, despite the odds being against it. As they approached the temple, the townsfolk scurried in and priest shut the door behind them. The gang looked around to see what the commotion was all about and heard heavy footsteps coming their way. They dismounted and hid behind a large hedge. Staring through the leaves, Stinu could see a brown horse's leg the size of a man. The creature growled, and it turned round, he saw it had one eye the middle of its forehead. It was a cyclops. It roared again, peering in the windows of the deserted houses. He went from house to house and when he found them empty; he left. The gang waited five more minutes and then they knocked on the temple door, but nobody answered.

"I think they are too frightened to come out," Vernu said.

"Yes. I can hardly blame them. Come on, let's see if we can stay out of his way, but if we do need to fight him, we will."

"He could have friends, you know," Ali said.

"If it comes to that, I think we can deal with it. I have a few tricks up my sleeve," Tina said. They got back on their horses. A three-hour journey brought them to another temple with an enormous staircase in front of it. When they reached the top of the stairs, they found the elaborate temple empty. The walls depicted crude paintings fighting beasts with spears and shields. The ground was littered with gold, trinkets and weapons.

"I don't think we have one of these," Ali said, picking up a spear with a lead tip. "I think it would come in handy." "I will take something with me to pay off Khalid." Then he saw a gold necklace with a large ruby in the middle. He picked it up and showed to Stinu.

Stinu smiled. "A necklace fit for a King, lad."

"Yes," Ali said, and punched the air with his fist.

"Give that to me, lad, and I will present it to Khalid at the right time." Stinu said.

"Okay, it's a deal," Ali said and handed over the trinket. Stinu nodded and placed it in his shoulder bag.

The others picked up lead spears of their own.

Once they had eaten, they retired for the evening. The following day, they were woken by a roaring lion and then the sound of fire. They ran to the entrance and faced a Chimera.

It had the head of a lion, the body of a goat and the tail of a Sorapis (snake) it saw them and breathed fire again, narrowly missing Stinu.

They attacked it with their swords, but were no match for it. They tried spears, but the Sorapis snapped toward them. The battle raged on and their arrows, swords and catapults had no effect and the conflict exhausted them.

And then Ali was pinned to the ground. He waited until it breathed fire again and jammed his lead spear into the creature's throat. The lead melted, and the monster died. His armour was singed, but he was unharmed. Tina helped him up.

"Thank you. It might be an idea to pick up weapons from ruins more often."

"Anything that will give us an edge has to be a good thing," Vernu said.

They pressed on sunset and the caught sight of the cyclops. He was eating one sheep from his flock. The travellers tried to be quiet, but he saw them and imprisoned them in his cage.

Chapter Twenty Four

Nadal had caught up with the heroes and he watched them go after the cyclops. Having an idea, using materials from his ship, he set up a market stall outside the village temple. Folks filtered out of the temple and children ran to the stall selling sweets, pastries and cakes, begging their mothers for money.

"Come and buy, come and buy. My sweets and cakes are the best in town," Nadal said with raised arms and twirling his staff above his head.

The adults viewed him with suspicion and tried his treats first before letting their children have any. Delighted eyebrows, gave way to quick sales and when Nadal had sold out, the village was under his control.

"These people are tricksters. And we must stop them," Nadal said from the front of the temple. "They are only in it for themselves. With your help I will rid the island of them and that wretched cyclops."

The crowd cheered, with whoops, yeahs, and whistles. Others talked amongst themselves, nodding in agreement.

"Let's take up arms and chase them away. If some or all of them die, you will thank me for it!" More cheering and the folks grabbed swords, torches, spears, axes and anything they could get their hands on and marched behind Nadal.

With clinched teeth and a sweating brow, Tina worked the lock on the cage. This was her fourth and final attempt. Success! The lock popped open, and they tiptoed towards the sleeping cyclops. His arm was resting on a chest with their weapons in it. The air smelt of sulphur and the sky had a thick orange hew. They heard lava bubbling. They were metres away now, and Tina threw a stone in front of the cyclops. His eye flickered open, and he rang to investigate. They retrieved their weapons from the chest and prepared for battle. He bellowed and his flock of sheep ran away.

"I've got an idea. Over here you one eyed wonder," Tina yelled, waving her arms. The cyclops saw her and ran over. She positioned herself over lava and threw a firework. The firework let off a white flare, and the cyclops was blinded and stumbled into the burning liquid. The cyclops tried to free himself but sizzled away to nothing. They mounted their horses and galloped away from danger. With the chaos behind them, they came to a serene and beautiful blue lake, surrounded by pine trees. They saw human shapes tying up canoes. They approached them and after haggling, they were paddling down the lake.

"I see you've been busy in your lab again, Tina," Vernu said, drawing alongside her canoe.

"Oh, I never stop, but are you referring to anything specifically?"

"That firework thing you used back there; quick thinking on your part."

"Thank you. I have some left. I'll give you some when we stop. You're no different; always trying to come up with the tasty dish."

"I guess that's why we get along."

"It could well be. Cooking isn't the only thing you practise. Your marksmanship is sublime."

"You're too kind. I think I have a bit of a small island mentality, but in a good way. I would listen to my husband's stories and I was always on guard. It was only a matter of time before our island was invaded and one day, our worst nightmare came true."

"I don't remember reading about it in a history book."

"You wouldn't be able to. It was a three-day skirmish our enemies were keen to bury. The Surinians attacked us, but our spies had done their job and we annihilated them."

Tina's eyes were wide, and her mouth formed a large O.

"Wow. They are a massive nation. How did you beat them?"

"I told you I am sworn to secrecy. Just like everyone else who was around," She said and then picked up speed, leaving the younger woman behind.

Tina allowed her oars to sooth her and watched as the flying fish leapt over her head and landed safely on her left. There was a heavy mist on the lake, but she wasn't bothered. For a moment, it was her, the lake and her little canoe. They reached the shore of the lake where Vernu was waiting for them. The horses got out of the lake and shook themselves off. They neighed playfully after enjoying their swim. Elk moved in the distance and Vernu shot one down. Then she prepared venison stuffed with rosemary and garlic with a red wine sauce and potatoes and game veg. They moved through the beautiful pines and clear lakes. They passed a waterfall, and they saw beavers, rabbits and deer playing in the wilderness. As they got closer to the waterfall, they could see fields upon fields of lilac crocuses. Saffron, the ingredient they came for. Before they could gather the spice, a centaur stopped them blocking their path. Everyone put their hands on their swords. The centaur clucked his tongue.

"That isn't very welcoming, is it?" He said.

"Nor is blocking our path," Tina said.

"All that you see here belongs to me. I will let you gather as much as you want; on one condition."

"And what condition is that?" Ali said.

"I would like you to answer three riddles and I will let you harvest until your heart's content. If you get them wrong, I will fight you to the death; and you will lose."

"I think we could take you without too much trouble. We don't have to listen to this!" Vernu said, drawing her sword. The centaur reared up, his eyes flashed and his nostrils flared.

"Do not provoke me, or you will pay the consequences. I am reasonable centaur and I will keep my word. This is your final warning!"

"She meant no harm," Stinu said. "Vernu put your sword away." Vernu re-sheathed her sword and the centaur relaxed.

"I am glad we can agree. Here is the first riddle: What gets bigger the more you take away?" the centaur said, digging a hole whilst the group huddled.

"Do you think we can trust that weirdo?" Ali said.

"What makes you think he's weird?" Stinu said.

"Have you looked at him? He can't decide if he is a man or a horse!"

"Point taken, let's concentrate. What gets bigger the more you take away?" he repeated.

"I don't think he is as bad as we think. He's digging a hole and I think that's the answer," Tina said, watching the centaur dig. The whole was a metre deep and a metre wide. Stinu looked over and the centaur was circling his handiwork.

"Is everyone certain, that the answer is a hole?"

"Yes," they said.

"I have to hurry you!"

Stinu turned to face the centaur.

"We think the answer is a hole."

The centaur trotted over and regarded them through squinted eyes. He circled twice, and then he stopped.

"Correct!" He said and flashed them a big smile. He almost looked cute!

He trotted some more, neighed, shook his head and scraped the ground with his front legs.

"Riddle number two: I can't go up but I can go down, but there is water all around. What am I?" As the group huddled again, he gazed at the waterfall.

Tina repeated the riddle this time.

"I think it's something to do with nature," Vernu said

"Do we chance it and have a look at what he's staring at?" But as Ali finished talking, the centaur circled them again.

"We saw a waterfall when we came in. I wonder if it's that," Tina said.

"Yes, it has to be!" Stinu said, snapping his fingers with an excited look on his face. "Are we all agreed?"

"Yes, we agree. We think the answer is waterfall."

"We are sure the answer is waterfall," Vernu said, before Stinu could say anything. He closed his mouth and scowled at her.

"I was going to say that!"

"We're a team. It doesn't matter who gives the answer, all that matters is getting the right one,"

"I guess," he said, folding his arms across his chest, bottom lip sticking out.

"That is the right answer!" The centaur said, and shot off down the track, leaving a dust cloud behind him. The others stood frowning after him.

"Ali, you were right. He *is* weird!"

"Maybe I am not such a poor judge of character."

"No one said you were," Tina said.

"Thanks for the compliment."

The centaur returned and rested his hand on a rundown wooden shack, whilst he got his breath back.

"And the third and final riddle," He said, in between breaths.

"Now you see me, now you don't. A flick of the tongue and I am a ghost!" "What am I?"

"Ah, he would have to save the hardest one for last, wouldn't he?" Stinu said.

"We need to think very hard before we answer this time," Ali said.

"I think it's something that can disappear," Tina said.

"I think you have just described Nadal, but I doubt that's the answer he's looking for!" And they all laughed.

"What about some kind of animal?" Vernu said.

"I am drawing a blank," Ali said.

"A chameleon!" Vernu and Tina said at the same time with excited eyes.

"A chameleon," Ali said, with a puffed chest and smug grin. The women protested.

"Silence!" The centaur said. He knitted his brow and circled for thirty seconds before answering. "Corrrrect!" He said and danced like he was a foal again.

"Congratulations. You may pick your saffron now." He said, letting them pass.

"I owe you an apology," Vernu said and held out her hand. The centaur looked at her hand and hugged her instead. Vernu hesitated and then she hugged him back. Then they let go.

"I understand I look a little intimidating, and I am sorry I couldn't give you the clue for the chameleon. They don't live around here, funnily enough!" And they both laughed. "Riddles are a code of honour for centaurs. If we can't learn to use them, they can banish us from our community. I will tell you about that when we get to the riddle tree. If you will permit me, I will show you my village. Don't worry, I won't give you more riddles or threaten you."

The others looked at each other and nodded.

"We'd love to join you," Vernu said.

"Splendid. I'll let you carry on."

An hour of back-breaking work gave them all the saffron they needed. The crew offered to pay Henry, but he refused. He talked the whole time they worked and told them his name. They rode to his village.

It was at the bottom of a small hill. They were rows of round thatched cottages and there were male and female centaurs and children played with toy bows and arrows.

The older children practiced with the real thing in a field behind the village, every one of them a crack shot.

Vernu watched with intrigue and realised that they may have lost a fight with Henry.

The village was bustling. There was the sound of industry in motion everywhere. Spinning wheels span, blacksmiths ground their stones and the smell of bread wafted on the breeze.

"They live in houses," Ali whispered to Tina.

"What, did you expect them to live in stables?"

"That's exactly what I expected."

"Really? You need to let go of your prejudices."

"I didn't know what to expect to be honest, but they seem to be very resourceful and civilised." A young female, about Ali's age, looked at him and then looked away again with a shy smile on her face.

"And I didn't expect that!"

"Pretend you're with me," Tina said and linked her arm with his. The female blushed and joined the archery field.

"And here we are," Henry announced. They were next to a large oak tree in the middle of a field. "This is the riddle tree!" He said with pride.

"Does the tree give you the riddles?" Tina said.

"No, I wish that was the case. They require us to come here for inspiration. We sit in the tree." He climbed up and sat on the lowest branch. "And let our minds dream up the riddles."

"Do you have to use different riddles every time?" Vernu asked.

"No, that isn't necessary but we like to challenge ourselves."

"You said they can banish centaurs from your community. Does that happen often?" Stinu asked.

"It is very rare for that to happen. When we are young foals, our teachers tell us about Sammy the stupid."

"He didn't like riddles and thought they were silly. He refused to learn them, and he was under constant supervision from the elders."

"On the open road, people would want to pick saffron, just like you did. Most of the time, we made our riddles easy to solve. I made yours harder because you looked smart. Sammy would tell the travellers the answers, making a mockery of the elder and our culture."

"You told us the answers for our riddles," Tina said.

"They allow us to offer clues, but we mustn't tell people the answers. Sammy told more and more travellers and one day bandits killed an elder and Sammy ran back to the village, screaming. His parents pleaded with the council not to send him away, but he was deemed a dangerous person and was forced out of town and was ordered to never return."

"A lesson to wayward centaurs everywhere," Ali said.

"Yes, quite so. Ah, Escobar. He looks troubled." The gang looked around and saw a black-haired centaur speeding towards them.

"A tall thin, stranger with a dark beard wearing purple robes, is leading an angry mob," Escobar said in between breathes. "And a cyclops seems to with them."

"How far away are they?"

"About a mile," Escobar said.

"That sounds like Nadal. He has a mind control potion, and I bet he is using it on the mob. Here, take these," Tina said, handing Henry a bottle of antidote and a copy of the recipe. "This will break the spell of the potion and the parchment shows you how to make more."

"Thank you. This is not your battle to fight; you must leave here."

"Trouble has a knack of following us around. We're not going anywhere. Nadal has been trailing us from the start and we led him to you. We need to put that right." Stinu said.

"I will do the best that I can but cannot guarantee your safety."

"We know the risks," Ali said.

"Wait, I have an idea," Vernu said and made them all gather in a huddle.

Invaders peered from left to right, but it was still in the centaur village. But every now and again, the silence was broken by the sound of cyclops footsteps.

An invader backed up a stairwell, and an arm reached out and pulled him inside the cottage. Stinu prised open the man's mouth and poured antidote down his throat, then knocked him out.

Another intruder walked past a stable, and Ali grabbed him and administered the cure to him. And so it went on until only Nadal and the cyclops were left. A short time passed, and the invaders were in their right minds again, and they circled Nadal and the beast.

"You tricked us," a man yelled.

"Yeah, you used our children to get to us and made us your slaves," another shouted. They drew closer and Nadal looked from left to right as the crowd advanced. Then he raised his arm in the air and threw something on the ground and a puff of blue smoke. He was gone. The cyclops stared and then roared. Henry trotted up to him.

"I command you to go or you will suffer the consequences."

The cyclops laughed, and the ground shook. Then he charged and tried to wrestle Henry, but Henry punched the cyclops in the eye and the creature stumbled backwards.

Centaurs fired arrows and threw spears, but the cyclops snapped at them like toothpicks. A punch winded Henry, and the cyclops pinned him to the ground. Henry flung some mud at his attacker, blinding him. His arms flailed about wildly and he stepped backwards onto a trip wire. The trap sprang and six spears from above fastened him to the ground.

A death rattle came from his throat, and his tongue drooped down the side of his face. His eyes fixed in a permanent stare. The four adventurers helped Henry to his feet.

"Thank you."

"Are there anymore cyclops out there? We also killed one," Ali asked.

"There are a few, but if you killed one, then they will think twice about attacking again. They are a dying out in these parts, thankfully. We will supply your country with as much saffron as you need. You can always count on us."

Vernu looked surprised.

"Are you sure? It's very expensive," She said.

"It is our pleasure. We are friends and allies. If you need our help I battle, send a carrier pigeon and we will rush to your aid." He snorted and puffed his chest, placing a fist over his heart.

"I was wrong about you Henry and your race. I hope you will accept my sincerest apologies," Ali said and offered his hand.

"Handshakes are so formal. Let's have a group hug instead." They hugged and then they said their goodbyes and the adventurers went back to the ship.

The moon replaced the sun, and they watched the dark waters lap against the side of the boat.

"That was a damn fine hot chocolate, mum."

"I am glad you liked it. You had to have two to be totally sure, didn't you?"

"We went through on Cyclops Island, it's nice to still be alive and enjoy hot chocolate."

"I'll drink to that," Stinu said, finishing his beverage.

"Me too!" Tina said, and she and her father thrust their mugs towards Vernu.

"Argh, sometimes I wish I wasn't so good at my job. Two more hot chocolates coming up!"

Ali waggled his cup.

"You've had enough, my boy," She said, disappearing down the stairs. Stinu and Tina laughed.

"It's not fair," Ali said, sticky out his bottom lip.

The others laughed all the more and Ali stomped down the stairs.

Chapter Twenty Five

A boisterous wind blew, and the ship lurched to the left. He sprang to his feet and put on his boots, and then he raced up the stairs.

"Captain, we are struggling to keep her under control," able sailor Dimitri.

"Replace the sails with the Jib and the storm trysail," Stinu said.

"Righto, sir," and he gave the order to the night crew.

The ship see-sawed as if it was a giant's plaything and tumultuous skies thundered with laughter, and lightning bolts pierced the clouds as if they were electric javelins. Salty gales stung Stinu's skin. A Huge wave pounded the vessel as he tried to regain control. A lurch flung men like rag dolls and they vomited.

"Trim the jib to the wind," he barked, and the sailors repeated the order. With all his strength, he turned the wheel away from the storm's deadliest, path. They were in open waters, no perilous rocks to deal with. An enormous wave rocked the boat, but Stinu steered the boat away from the worst of the storm.

"Deploy sea anchor," he yelled and as they did, the boat slowed and they sailed on calmer waters. He and his crew had done it.

Tina came from below deck, and her father greeted her with a weary smile. He had dark circles under his eyes and his hair was messier than normal. The tranquil sea and warm sun made the sailors look like liars.

"Here, drink this," she said, handing him a strong coffee. "When you finish this go to bed. I'll take the helm."

After he drained the scolding liquid, he smacked his lips and slouched back to his bed.

***

"I have never met a centaur before," Vernu said. She had finished the breakfast shift and watched Tina.

"Nor have I. I had heard stories but didn't know what to expect. Were you impressed with their archery skills?"

"Yes, and intimidated. Let's just say I am glad they are the good guys."

"Oh, make no mistake, if they don't like you, you'll know. Henry and his village seemed friendly, but they knew how lucrative saffron would be."

"Don't you trust them?"

"I think they will be fine, but centaurs are shrewd and clever creatures. They know how to watch out for number one. They are noble and they stick to their word. I praise the Lord it worked out okay for us."

"Amen to that. How long before we reach Timun?"

"Should be there in four hours."

"That's not too long. What do you make of this tribe that crossbreeds animals?"

"Is there any truth in that?" Tina said, making a face.

"Nothing would surprise me at this point. We only need two more ingredients."

Tina nodded. "Would you do it all again?"

"I am sure we will. The old book isn't complete we need to find the rest of it,"

"For what it's worth, you're right, the book is important. To us, to Tarnuz and the world,"

"Wow, that is a big vision you have there!"

"Dream big or go home!"

"A bold statement, but I like it!"

They smiled. And they reminisced about home, and the hours passed by like minutes. Then Tina thought she saw something.

"Take the wheel, keep her steady," she said, handing her the wheel and then opening her telescope. A rocky skull rose out of the sea like a gothic scarecrow, and Tina wondered how many curious sailors had lost their lives.

"Land ho," she yelled and rang the bell, and then the crew rushed into position to prepare to anchor the ship. Stinu and Ali appeared and with minutes, gang were rowing to the shore in silence. Nobody voiced their thoughts, and the skull made Ali shudder.

Lord, we need your peace in this situation. It chills my soul. He prayed in his head.

This isn't the end. I need to deal with Nadal and Khalid, but this is not Bruno's home anymore and I sense something evil. Help us overcome evil with good. Amen. Was Stinu's silent prayer.

Help us, Lord, get what we came for. Amen. Tina prayed.

I am putting my trust in you, Lord. I have no one else to turn to. Vernu prayed. The boat came to rest on dark sand and the magenta sky was a beautiful but unsettling sight and Ali's stomach flipped.

"How could I be so stupid?" Someone said. It the voice sounded like rocks sliding down a cliff.

The adventurers looked at each other.

"Where did that voice come from?" Vernu said

"I think it came from over there, Ali said, pointing at a gap between mountains.

"I'll go and investigate," Ali said.

"Don't you want us to help you, lad?" Stinu said.

"If I'm not back in ten minutes, come and find me."

"See you soon," Tina said.

He scratched the back of his neck, and cleared his throat.

"See you in ten," he said trying to sound brave.

Sweeping away branches, he saw a foot made of rock. The foot was wedged in a cave mouth.

"Little boy. Can you help me?"

The rock voice spoke again. Ali gazed at the foot and his eyes travelled up the foot, up the leg and eventually found the face. Every body part was made of rock.

A man made out of rock! Interesting!

"My name is Petram. Both my feet are wedged in holes and I can't bend down far enough to unhook them. If you help me I will help you. I feel so silly. I have been walking this land five hundred years and this has never happened before."

"My name is Ali. Let me inspect your feet." He inspected both feet and realised that Tina's exploding catapult bolts would free him.

"Petram, I need help from my friends. I'll be right back."

"I can't move so I will wait here for you."

"Okay see you soon," Ali said.

The others were relieved to see him safe and unharmed.

"Who did the voice belong to?" Vernu asked.

"Promise not to laugh," he replied.

"We promise," They said.

"A rock giant has trapped both of his feet in caves!"

Tina sniggered but pretended to sneeze.

Stinu bit into his fist.

Vernu smiled.

"I know what to do," Vernu said testing the sling on her catapult.

"So do I," Tina said, copying Vernu's actions.

"That's exactly what I had in mind," Ali said.

Moving to the right foot, Vernu fired an exploding bolt. Rocks tumble and Petram pulled his foot free. Another bolt was fired by Tina and Petram was freed.

"Thank you all so much. If you ever need my help, just yell my name and I will be there.

"Thank you, Petram."

"I continue to marvel at this world," Stinu said.

"As do I, father," Tina said, and stood on tiptoes and kissed him on the cheek.

"I still feel uneasy about this place," Ali remarked.

"Me too," Vernu said.

Stinu and Tina nodded.

"Very nice to meet you all," Petram said. "And a million thanks for helping me, but I'll be off now."

"Can you stay for a bit? " I feel uneasy, like there is something evil approaching."

"Very well," Petram sighed, and the trees shook from his breath.

Cautiously, they moved further onto the island and came to a lake; Petram's footsteps shaking the ground. Ali gripped his sword tighter for confidence. Vernu had her bow loaded, and the gang ambled off the beach. Tina swapped her stone hatchet from hand to hand and Stinu held his sword ready to strike. A strong wind blew through the trees and the grass. A dark shadow passed over them and they could hear large wings flapping. Something exhaled, and the ground caught fire. A foul stench clogged the air. Their eyes streamed, and they coughed and gagged. Ali peered through sore eyes and saw a dragon fly over a lake. The beast came to rest on a mountain facing the lake, its mouth open in a grin.

"That doesn't look good at all. Can't we find bay leaves somewhere else, somewhere without DRAGONS!" Ali said.

"We have some at home, but Khalid won't let us use them." Vernu said.

"That's not a choice, then!"

"How can we kill the beast?" Stinu said.

"Quite often it has a source of power. We need to find out what," Tina volunteered.

The dragon attacked Stinu and his trousers caught fire. He writhed around the ground and Tina filled a bucket of water and threw it over him. The dragon pulled itself up and away from the lake.

"Are you okay, Dad?"

"Yes, I'll be fine, thanks."

Tina sighed, and they hugged.

"I have an idea. Everyone stand in front of the lake. We need to make the dragon furious."

"Are you sure you know what you are doing, mum?"

"I don't have a clue. Anybody else?"

They all shook their heads. They stood with the lake behind them, and when the dragon swooped down again, they threw every weapon they had at it. As the dragon breathed, they dived out of the way as its flames licked lake.

Ali looked the rock giant in the face. "Petram, I think we have a bit of a dragon problem here." Ali said. "Do you think you could deal with it?"

"No worries, a promise is a promise," He bellowed, folding his arms across his chest.

As the dragon flew past, Petram grabbed its tail and, tucked the beast under his arm right arm and squeezed the dragon's back like a set of bellows, flames spurting out of his mouth. The dragon's eyes bulged with each squeeze and returned to their sockets when Petram let go. Moving towards the lake, Petram directed the jets of fire across the water and the water started to smell.

The foul odour consumed the water, and the dragon's colour drained away. He turned from red to white. Petram tied the dragon in a knot and threw him at the stinking venomous lake. The poisonous gas claimed its victim.

They thanked Petram. He waved and was gone.

Walking around the lake, they took shelter in a cave and set up camp.

Stinu warmed his hands by the fire, Tina rocked backwards and forwards in a blanket and Ali bothered the fire with a stick.

"I am going out," Stinu said, groaning as he got up, stretching his back.

"Okay, see you later," Vernu said, and carried on sharpening her knife.

It didn't take long for Stinu to find the winding mountain path. Night had descended, and it was as black as pitch. The night felt oppressive. Sweat trickled down his neck and his legs shook, but he pressed on regardless. Lightning sparked across the sky and the air smelt of Petrichor. Mud and sludge made his footsteps feel like someone had shackled him and the storm wasn't granting a reprieve. He slipped and fell on his back, sliding to the bottom of the hill. He winced from the pain in his back, but he regained his footing, he reached the top of the mountain, just as the clouds opened and the raindrops stung him like tiny darts from blow pipes. Planting his feet, he raised his trembling arms.

"I don't know if we can take anymore. I thank you for our safety so far and I am grateful. A lightning bolt struck the tree next to him and he dived to the ground, trembling; He got and up and continued his petition.

"I ask you to grant us safe passage on the rest of our quest. If we are on our last mission, I pray we will bring peace to Tarnuz," He bellowed, but the weather drowned out his pleas.

I am with you in the storm and the silence.

"Is that you, Lord? I expected a large audible voice." A few minutes passed and then the wind and rain receded, the clouds cleared and the stars and moon appeared. The satellite cast its light across the mountain, setting the prisoner free from a watery execution; he made his way back to the cave and collapsed in the entrance.

Foggy visions dance before his eyes and someone mopped his brow. They placed a bottle to his lips, and he gulped down the liquid. He propped himself up and stood. He swayed, but the others steadied him. Blinking, his vision cleared. Someone placed a wooden bowl in his hands and he could smell broth. He slurped down the food without apology and wiped his mouth with his sleeve.

"How long had I been out?"

"Just a few hours. I worried about you, Dad."

"By some miracle, you don't appear to have pneumonia," Vernu said.

"A miracle is what I have experienced. The Lord spoke to me in the storm!"
They turned to face him.

"What did he say?" Ali said with excitement.

"I travelled up the mountain and prayed. I thanked him for helping us so far and asked him he could keep us safe. Then he said: I am with you in the storm and the quiet times."

"Did he say it out loud? Did he shout?" Vernu said, eyes widening.

"No, neither. More of a voice inside my head." Vernu and Ali peeled away from him, and Tina averted her eyes. He looked at them for reassurance. "You think I am crazy I got poisoned, but I know what I heard!"

"The Lord said, stand on the mountain before me, and I will pass by."

"A powerful wind tore the mountains apart, shattering rocks before the Lord, but he was not there. An earthquake blew, but he had gone. Fire came, but he left. After the fire came a gentle whisper." "1 Kings 19:11," Tina said

Tina closed the book and smiled. Ali removed his hand from his chin and he and Vernu looked at Stinu with open mouths.

"Now do you believe me?" He said, folding his arms.

"I think it's undeniable. You heard from the Lord," Vernu said.

"Yes, I think he has more ways of talking!" Ali said. They all nodded. Fingers of sunlight stretched into the cave and birdsong drifted on the breeze.

"I am not crazy let the day begin. Stinu said, striding past them in fresh clothes and with renewed vigour. With a shrug, the others packed up and strode after him.

***

The drums grew louder, and the ropes tightened like a braided corset around his torso. Tribal dances made his temples throb. A snort prodded his feet with its tusks and wagged its tail. Nadal wriggled to catch his breath, and the ropes slipped a bit.

"There is an evil gang coming for you." He yelled, going red in the face. The chief held up a fist, and the ritual stopped. "I can help you defeat them."

"Cut him down," The chief said and rattled off words that Nadal didn't understand and a knife cut him free. He fell to his knees with a grunt and then his mouth curled into a wicked grin.

A dark mood still clouded Stinu's judgement, despite the encouragement on the mountain. Two storms in two days had shaken him. There was also the magenta sky. He liked magenta, but this place tightened his gut. It looked beautiful and but it felt hostile? He would be glad to leave the island.

I wonder if the Lord we speak like that again? Vernu thought. *It's a beautiful day but the birds aren't singing. This a beautiful meadow and no rabbits or hares play here. There is evil in this place!* Vernu thought.

After a days' travelling, the sun disappeared, and the shadows broadened. A salty breeze made their noses twitch, and the hills became cliffs. Vernu glanced left at the rocks. Someone had carved a statute of a man into them. The sound of drums grew louder. She looked over her shoulder and saw an immense crowd running towards them, sand and spray flying in their wake. Children were playing with a raft on her right.

"You may have cheated death many times before, but today you die!" Nadal yelled at them from the grassy clifftop, as he sprinkled a powder onto the statue. With a loud crack, the statue peeled away from the cliff.

"I am Bel Ebenniu, lord of the rocks, and I will kill you." The giant bellowed and threw a large rock in their direction, the impact sent them flying. Winded, but okay, they dropped everything but their weapons and run towards the children. The children abandoned their raft, and the adventurers clambered aboard and paddled with their hands as fast as they could. Another rock landed nearby but the gigantic wave helped them escape and they paddled harder until the tribe, Nadal and the rock giant were in the distance.

A full moon gave no comfort or guidance; its silvery beams melted into the sea, drowning their hopes. After drawing straws, Stinu took the first shift.

"It will not defeat me. We need bay leaves," he said, steering the raft towards the other side of the isle. It was a black, bony finger putting out to sea like a grave digger pointing out a grave.

"We need to land on the other side," He said, but snores answered him.

The merciless sun rose, and by noon, the makeshift headbands were useless. They floated closer to the island, but sun stroke made them weak.

Crash! The raft rammed into rocks and they woke up. They scrambled up the beach and collapsed into a cave. A drip of water woke Tina with a start. With every fibre of strength left in her body, she crawled around a slippery path and followed the sound of running water. It wasn't long before she found a small pool of water. She drank from it with cupped hands. It tasted good, and she drank and drank and drank, like a thirsty dog. She fetched the others, and they also drank.

After regaining her strength, Vernu killed some fish with her bow and she grilled them on the fire. Stinu gave them coconuts to drink and then they set out. Burning sunlight punished them like a wicked taskmaster, who was never satisfied. They found shade and considered their options. Tina got up and searched for water. Ten minutes later, she came to a water hole and a beautiful horse was lapping from a pool. She knelt down and lapped at the water.

"My name is Celer. What is your name?" The horse had multi-coloured lines moving across its body like streams of coloured water, beautiful and mesmerising at the same time.

"I am called Valentina and I need bay leaves!" She placed her hand over her mouth. Why did she say that? She splashed water on her face.

"Climb on my back. I will take you to them." Her limbs obeyed, but her mind objected. She held on tight and the horse started on the journey. Trees, plants, colourful flowers and exotic plants flashed by as the horse increased its speed. Images swam before her eyes and she went giddy. She gripped harder on the horse's mane and tried not to vomit as the speed increased. Pictures of her childhood mingled with Stinu, Vernu and Ali's faces. She saw giant spiders, cyclops, and harpies; laughter and tears and food. A vortex pulled at her body, threatening to carry her away. It swept trees and debris up with her, and her eyelids grew heavy. She reached behind her and touched the hilt of her dagger, but her fingers slipped. With one last attempt, she pulled the knife free and plunged it in the horse's neck. The animal slowed, and she twisted the beast towards a cold water lake. The creature tried to stop, but it was too late and the demon drowned. Tina swam to the shore and passed out. Through blurred vision, she saw the relentless sun. It had burnt her face. Her lips were chapped and dry.

After her eyes had focused, she saw a bay tree; a green beacon of hope in a desert of despair.

With every ounce of strength she crawled towards it, she took clippings and stumbled around the lake perimeter. After she had climbed the rocks, she found an opening and squeezed herself inside and waited for nightfall. A hoot of an owl made her jump, and she had neck cramp. She moved her head back and forth. Her leg had gone to sleep. She rubbed her leg and started crying.

Chapter Twenty Six

"We'll find her, Stinu," Vernu said, trying to sound positive, but sounded defeated.

"Where has she gone?" He asked, pacing the floor.

"Come and look at this," Ali said. They rushed over to see. He was studying the hoof marks and footprints. "I bet if we follow these, it will lead us right to her."

"Let's do it. I don't think we will get any sleep tonight, anyway."

They followed the tracks what felt like hours and then they reached the lake. They traced Tina's footsteps and started calling her name.

"I am up here," she called, and they followed the sound of her voice. They hugged and wept, they found a larger opening set up camp and slept. Morning rain lashed against the opening and they stood in it and let it soak them. Grey clouds replaced the rain, and they sat there in silence. Tina opened and closed her fist, staring at the bay leaves, but not caring. A dark shadow fell on them, followed by a familiar squawk. Zilli landed and Galaxio climbed down from his back.

"Boy am I glad to see you!" Stinu said, and hugged the assistant so hard, he gasped for breath!

"Great to see you too, Sir. Can you let me go now?"

"Oh, sorry yes, of course," he said and stepped back, releasing the man.

"I got back from nursing Zilli and the crew said they hadn't seen you for two days. I started searching for you straight away. Let's back to the ship. You look and stink like wet dogs!"

Nobody responded and climbed on the back of the gigantic bird. He circled and then flew them back to the ship.

Galaxio and his team cared for them for three days. They regained their strength. The salves helped cool their lips and heal their skin.

***

"That horse gave me the ride of my life and it could have been the ride of my death too!" Tina said, placing her playing card on the table.

"Snap!" Ali shouted; placing his card on top of hers and making everyone jump. He snatched the cards and grinned like a hyena. "Sorry, Tina. You were saying."

"Yes, I started telling you about that horse. I think he was a demon. He said his name was Celer, and I found myself hypnotised by his bright colours. I told him I needed bay leaves, and he offered to take me to them. I climbed on his back and he started speeding up. He ran faster and faster until he created a devastating vortex. Trees and rocks spun around me and I felt giddy and images from my life played in front of me."

They lent forward to hear more.

"What happened next?" Vernu said with a look of wonder.

"I stabbed the evil thing in the neck and drowned it in the lake." Stinu got up from the table and climbed above deck. Tina found him piloting the ship.

"I came so close to losing you today."

"You have come close to losing me every day."

"You know what I mean. Today was closer than others."

"Sometimes it's easy to forget the risks we take on dangerous missions."

"We got caught in the moment."

"Yes, we did"

"Mistress, Valentina, Master Cilistinu," Galaxio said, interrupting them. "Please join me at the kitchen table? Mistress Vernu and Master Alessandro have agreed."

"Sure, Galaxio, lead the way!" Stinu said.

Everyone listened as the servant filled them in on the events they had missed.

"Upon reaching Zilli's island, the bird healed fast, but he needed to regain his strength. Soon after he was strong again, he flew around with his relatives and had fun with them. I wasn't sure he would return, but after two days, he did and we flew towards the ship. When we found the Sibell, the crew told me you were missing, and they feared for your safety. I left to search for you straight away. I found your belongings on the beach where you left them. They are in chests over there," He said, pointing at them. The others put down their warm apple juice and looked behind them.

"Didn't Nadal and his tribe attack you?" Ali said.

Galaxio looked at the table and sighed.

"When we arrived, the tribe were dead and Nadal had gone."

No one spoke. Stinu gulped down his drink and Tina grimaced.

"I bet Nadal got away without a single scratch. He's as slippery as a Sorapis and twice as cunning," Vernu said.

"Yes. He won't stop until we are in prison or dead."

"Well, I hope that neither of those things happen," Ali said.

"I'd like to see him locked up. I will serve justice to him. King Stefano is a fair and just king, assuming we can regain control of the city," Stinu said.

"Do you doubt we can take it back?" Ali said.

"We only have one mission left before we return home, so it's likely we will succeed, but you never know for sure."

"Let's pray," Vernu said. "Lord, we thank you we escaped the island and we pray you will enable us to slay the giant lobster and give us wisdom on how to restore peace to Tarnuz. 'Amen."

"Amen," They echoed.

A boisterous wind howled around the vessel, and then a dull object hit the ship, tilting it to the right. With hard steps, they made it above deck and one sailor ran towards Stinu.

"Captain, we are being attacked by a huge squid!" He said, petrified.

"Captain, I have constructed a large harpoon device," Galaxio said.

"Very good Galaxio, load it and prepare to fire."

"You, you and you," Galaxio said, pointing at three sailors. "Help me load the harpoon" Galaxio and the three other sailors hoisted the harpoon on their shoulders and Stinu drew his knife.

Vast sea-green eyes looked at the captain and a feeler flicked out and grabbed him like a snake grabbing a mouse; it drew the man closer to its parrot mouth. Suckers slurped as they gripped him like tiny mouths. Its slimy red arrow tip head glistened in the sunlight. Like a spider in a web, it tightened its hold on its prey, and the intense pain choked a scream in his throat. More tentacles curled around his body, like boa constrictors, and Stinu could see row upon row of sharp teeth. Jaws gnashed, and Stinu's face felt like it was going to burst. The monster's eyes were deceptive. They looked innocent and harmless, but its body had scars of war. It had one weakness, and Stinu knew what it was. It wasn't the limbs; they were as pliable as leather. It was the head. With a charging bull, or a giant squid it needs to lower its head to strike. The creature relaxed its grip and Stinu made his move. He slashed at its neck and it recoiled. As he fell, the harpoon entered the wound and the sea vampire lost its head. Sailors caught their captain, and the slain animal slipped into the water. Sharks tore at its body as the ship sailed on.

With a hand on his chest, Stinu tried to regain his breath. They slid a chair under him and he wheezed as his breathing levelled out. Burn marks had appeared on his arms and legs, and his chest felt tight. Men ushered him to his bed and Tina, Vernu and Ali gathered at his side.

"I came close to losing you today," Tina said, tears pooling in her eyes.

Stinu choked out a laugh.

"I didn't want you to feel left out!"

She sobbed a laugh, and the others turned theirs into a cough.

"Can I see the patient?" Galaxio said, and they let him through.

"Everything looks in order. Rest for two days," he said, after he had examined him.

"Thank you, Galaxio," Tina said, clasping his hands in hers. "You have been a real asset to us. I don't know how we could have lived without you," She said, leaning forward and kissing his cheek. He blushed.

"Right you are. Let me know if you need anything." And then he left.

Sometimes, sick people could pick their meal of choice. Stinu wanted steak, but Vernu declined.

"You won't be able to chew it and I don't have any. And I'll cook it for you when we're in Tarnuz, promise. We'll all have it. I'll make chicken instead."

"Okay, I won't let you forget,"

"Nor will we," Ali and Tina said, and they laughed.

"I have remembered something about gruff voice man," Ali said, and Stinu sat up in bed.

"Go, lad, tell us, the Admiral enquired.

"I think he was weighing coins."

Stinu clicked his fingers.

"That sounds like Clepta, the head of the royal mint!" "We need to question him. This could be our chance to over throw Nadal." Stinu said, and then he coughed and clutched his throat. It hurt when he talked.

"Yes Nadal is a monster, and he must be stopped." Ali replied.

"Sometimes the monsters we fight are too powerful for us and I fear they will overcome us," Ali said.

"That had occurred to me, too. I am hoping the next mission won't be too soon after this. I have some interesting prototypes I want to test first."

Ali lent back as Vernu placed mugs of hot chocolate in front of them. The sweet aroma made Ali feel hungry and sleepy all at once.

"Tell me more."

"Like I said, they are prototypes. I don't want to get people's hopes up. I could end up blowing myself up!"

"Lots of little Tina's around. As if one isn't enough," he said, and she kicked him in the shin, and he spilt his chocolate down his tunic.

"Aw, that hurt!"

"Good, you'll have more respect next time!"

"You would have said the same thing."

"Maybe," she said, twirling her hair around her finger.

"What do you miss most about Tarnuz?" he said, changing the subject.

"Ooo, loads of things, but my nice cosy bed, would be top."

"Ah, yes, that is good. I miss mine too."

"Your turn."

"I already mentioned the pink ices, didn't I?"

"Yes, you did."

"I thought so." He leaned forward and Tina did too. "I like the steak and gravy pies the pie seller sells in the market," he said, in hushed tones. 'I think if mum found out, she'd be cross,'

"She already knows," Vernu said, making Ali jump. She stood in front of him, wringing a cup with a tea towel like she was throttling a chicken, eyes blazing. Ali gulped. And then she laughed and slapped her thigh. Tina burst into laughter and stood next to Vernu, bumping into each other like a pair of drunken sailors.

"I feel like they have set me up," he said, folding his arms.

"We have set you up!" Tina said, pointing at him and collapsing with laughter.

"Listen, listen, Ssh," Vernu said. "I supply the guy at the market with pies!" And the two women carried on laughing. Ali waited until they had composed themselves before he spoke.

"I am pleased you are laughing."

"Really? Why?" Vernu said.

"Well, it's been a while since we've all had a great laugh."

The two women looked surprised.

"No, I mean it."

"Yes. It has been a while," Tina said.

"There you go. I am going to help the sailors." He downed his drink, grabbed a mop and bucket and moved upstairs.

Chapter Twenty Seven

A scraping sound ground the ship to a halt.

"Abandon ship, abandon ship," one sailor yelled.

"Curses, I am so close to my goal," Nadal said. "And now Stinu and his band of fools have gone I can implement the last part of my plan."

"Sir, we must get you to safety. We are taking on a lot of water. Follow me, your lifeboat is waiting."

"Very well, lead the way." They led him to the boat and lowered it to the sea. Other boats joined them, and the crew rowed to the shore. Some watched over their shoulders as the large boat creaked and moaned and sank.

Sea creatures would make it their home as the waters claimed another victim, a relic of its former self. It would become a museum, a treasure waiting to be discovered. With one eye to his telescope, Nadal watched his possessions plummet to the bottom of the ocean. There were copies of his potion books on Tarnuz, but his research was lost forever and he felt a pain in his heart, but he would keep his defeat to himself. Weakness was not a choice. Love died with Marvello, and he hardened his heart. He gripped his robes, and he wanted to tear them, but he wouldn't let his emotions control him. His telescope scanned the harbour. An unexpected shallow rock formation had scuppered the ship, so they were only a mile from the shore. Tiny stick figures busied themselves with market day. Fishermen stacked lobster pots, greengrocers prepared their wares for the day, bakers arranged bread and sweet pastries, and cloth merchants draped fine silks over poles. The market was a hive of activity. A gentle tap on the quayside announced their arrival, and they disembarked. After they secured Nadal on dry land, one of the crew handed him a note.

"What's this you have given me?"

"It's bad news, master. We intercepted a carrier pigeon with this attached to it."

The paper had the royal seal on it.

Although we had a slight altercation with an enormous sea monster, the winds are with us and we are making excellent progress. We should dock within two days. We look forward to exchanging stories upon our return. Kind regards, Cilistinu, Captain by Royal appointment.

The letter was three days old. They were ahead. A gritted growl emitted from his mouth and he screwed up the note and threw the note into the emerald sea. The harbour was bustling with life. It was peaceful, but it didn't work on Nadal.

"We need, need, to, find a ship," a prodding finger punctured every word in the message bearer's chest. "Cilistinu and his merry band are a day ahead of us. We need to stop them! Get me a ship! At a good price! Chop! Chop!" he said, clapping his hands together, and sailors scurried like rats searching for suitable vessels to take them home.

Chapter Twenty Eight

They stood a better chance of infiltrating the city at night. Vernu, to everyone's surprise, had come up with the plan. Stinu and some crew had protested, but the chef revealed her hand.

Before she married Ali's father, she was a royal spy. They worked together when the king needed intelligence on an enemy. She served the king for five years, then she found out she was pregnant. After that, she changed careers.

"Brilliant," Ali said.

"What is?"

"Sending the note later."

"Thank you. I had a hunch that Nadal would intercept it, so making him think we were dead a little longer, has bought us time," Stinu said, whilst continuing to row.

They decided it would be two teams of four. Stinu lead one team and Vernu lead the other. It was 3A.M., three and a half hours before sunrise. A few lamps flickered in windows as the teams secured their boats. The skyline was littered with buildings of different shapes and sizes. Some spires had star and moon weather veins. Others had tear drop shapes. A city mourned for its brainwashed inhabitants. Everything was still.

"Good luck," Vernu whispered, and both teams hugged and went their separate ways. Stinu and Ali's team moved right and Vernu and Tina's to the left. Clepta's house was a five-minute walk from the dock, and they tiptoed to the rear. Ali picked the lock and opened the door quietly. A brief whiff of wine escaped as they entered the room and the torch's flame picked out wine bottles lying on shelves, like sleeping guests after a drunken dinner party. There was a staircase to their left.

"You two stay here. Ali and I will deal with the forger," Stinu whispered, and the sailor nodded. With soft and careful steps, the two men navigated the building. They crept on the wooden floorboards; they came to two dark wooden doors. Stinu pressed his ear to the right door, Ali took the left. Ali shook his head and Stinu did likewise. They moved to Ali's left across a short landing to a staircase in the middle. They walked cautiously to a door. Stinu placed his ear to it and he nodded. With a delicate touch, he lifted the latch and entered the room. Clepta snorted and rolled on his side. The smell of sweat hung in the air. His hand hung out of the bed. An empty wine bottle rolled away from his twitching fingers. Ali pushed Clepta's hand and his eyes flickered open. Feeling the tip of Stinu's blade on his neck, he gulped in terror.

"Get up and keep quiet. You don't want to get blood on your silk sheets, do you?" He shook his head and got out of bed. Ali bound his hands behind his back with rope and then he pushed him forward and the man grunted.

"You can have all of my money. I'll show you where."

Stinu snorted and exhaled.

"You are the best forger in the country; I am not interested in your money. I how will I know if it's real? Get down stairs." When he was in the wine cellar, they tied him to a chair. "Clepta, I want you to tell me about this scheme you have with Nadal. Try not to miss anything out; I have little patience with traitors!" He said, placing his boot on the man's thigh, aiming his sword at his throat.

Chapter Twenty Nine

Sleep darts took care of the two guards patrolling the royal well, and Vernu's team tied and gagged them, hiding them from view. Then they rolled a wooden beer barrel filled with Tina's antidote over to the well. All four of them lifted the barrel and emptied the contents into the water supply. Nadal had polluted the water supply with his mind control potion. There were three wells left: East, south and west. The wells didn't have a guard, and by morning, everyone would be free of Nadal's power. This carried on for five nights, and then the team revealed themselves.

***

The Sebi was half the size of the Sibell, a fast fishing vessel used in lobster catching.

Ali and both teams poised with spears tipped with sleeping darts. They needed the lobster alive.

Lobster was a delicacy, but it didn't start out that way. Peasants used to find them washed up on the shore. If they ended up in prison, they were fed them. This was before everyone labelled them vermin. People decided they were the sea's equivalent of rats, the scavengers of the sea, clearing away the rubbish. They tasted okay, but one day, a live one fell into a pot and the chef ate it when it finished cooking. The flavour was sublime, and he persuaded others to eat it and its popularity grew and it became a rich person's food.

As they drew close to the giant lobster feeding ground, Ali peered in the turquoise sea. A purple blue crustacean swam close to the ship. It had a thin body and a hard shell. Its body had three segments, and it had a fan-shaped tail.

Ali clutched his spear harder and his hands turned white.

"We're going to need a... whoa," He said as the lobster tapped the vessel, knocking him overboard. He stabbed the lobster with his spear and pulled himself up with it. "Whatever you do," was all he said, as the lobster surfaced and submerged again.

"Do it," he said, before he disappeared again. The lobster rose again, and Tina's spear found its mark. The lobster thrashed a bit, but they needed more spears. It was a colossal beast, six metres long; it would take four spears to knock it out. Ali rose again, but Stinu's spear missed. Third time, Vernu got a direct hit, and the lobster flagged and Ali leapt from its back and they helped him board. Bruno dealt the last blow and sailors dived in to retrieve their prize. Pulley ropes secured the beast and when they it lowered on the deck, they bound its claws. They poured ice cubes all over its body and they made the quick trip to the dock. When they arrived on dry land, they ran through the streets carrying the sea monster. People cleared a path as they rushed to the kitchen.

***

An hour later, Ali, Stinu and Tina were waiting outside the palace dressed in their best banqueting attire.

"Are you sure about this? I know how you felt about testing it on Bruno."

"I am sure. After you dad told me Bruno's backstory, the poor guy has been through enough."

"Fair point," She said, handing him the vial of the mind control potion. "Only two drops. We are trying to prove a point, nothing else."

"Believe me; I can't wait for this to be over!"

Stinu placed his hand on Ali's shoulder.

"We'll be praying in our heads for you," he whispered.

"Thanks," and the three of them hugged.

The royal trumpets sounded.

"Will all guests make their way to the banqueting hall, please?" The majordomo announced.

"This is it," Stinu said, and they all sat down.

Clepta sat next to Stinu.

"Do you need a recap?"

"I know what to do," I just hope that Bea will come back to me," he said.

"I am glad you understand. I can't make your wife return, but if you do the right thing today, I'll help you get her back." Stinu said, trying to reassure the forger.

"Thanks, Admiral. I will need all the help I can get."

"That you will my man, that you will," Stinu said patting the young man's hand.

"All rise for his royal highness, King Stefano!" Everyone got to their feet. Guests had come from far and wide. Stinu recognised members of King Khalid's royal detachment. Noble men from both countries, princesses giggling as handsome princes looked their way, court jesters and musicians, servers and servants, poured drinks for loud portly gentlemen and children well dressed and on their best behaviour. All stood to attention. The trumpets sounded, and Tarnuz's King entered the room followed by King Khalid. They took their seats next to each other and then the guests sat.

Music started and people resumed their conversations or drinking or both. The palace doors opened with a loud bang and the music stopped and everyone turned towards them. Nadal came through the doors and made his way to the King's table, but the guards stopped him and directed him to a table opposite. After a grumble, he sat down and King Stefano leaned over and whispered something into Khalid's ear and they both stared at him.

"Why am I being treated like a stray dog? I am the King's vizier. I demand to sit with my King!"

"Nadal, brother, I must remind you who you are addressing. "Let's eat," he said, and clapped his hands.

Servers and attendants came through the kitchen doors carrying a starter of chicken soup and crusty rolls. The main course of paella followed. Twelve servers carried the enormous lobster and everyone gasped as it made its way to the table. They gave plates to the two kings and everyone waited for the King to eat and then give his opinion. The King's chewing was the only sound and his face gave nothing away. He swallowed, sighed, and sat back in his chair.

"Most exquisite, you may eat." And everyone started tucking into their food. When everyone had eaten, the King addressed his audience.

"Would my intrepid explorers please stand?" Before he got up, Ali poured two drops of the potion in his goblet and drank. Somebody had fetched Vernu, and she straightened her dress and fixed her hair whilst standing next to Ali. She curtsied to the King out of respect and he smiled. Ali gave her wide eyes, and she stamped on his foot. His foot was painful, but he recovered.

"Please tell us about the conspiracies you have uncovered." The crowd gasped and muttered.

Tina performed a curtsey.

"Permission to speak, your highness," Tina said.

"You may speak."

"Thank you, your highness. Ali, get up and take the guard's sword." The potion had taken effect, and he did as he was told. The guard looked at the King.

"It's okay, George. It's just a demonstration." The solider relaxed and Ali took his sword.

"Ali, return the sword to its owner." Ali did as he was told. More gasps from the crowd.

"I would like to call another witness, sire."

"Of course, go right ahead."

"Thank you, my King. Clepta, please step forward." He stepped forward and stood next to her. "Please tell the King and everyone present if you have witnessed mind control before."

"Your Highness, I have seen this before."

"When did you see this?"

His eyes watered, and he looked at the ground.

"I saw Nadal use it on the royal kitchen staff. His mind control potion had worn off, and he had to give them a stronger dose."

The guests got restless and some shouted. The majordomo called for silence and calm returned.

"Did he use the potion on anyone else?"

"Yes, I believe he used it on the entire city." More outrage from the crowd. The majordomo banged a gong and people stared with wide eyes and open mouths.

"Mr Clepta, could you tell everyone what you do for a living."

"I work for the royal mint and I make fake Staters." The King banged his staff before the crowd acted up again.

"Can you show the difference between a fake coin and a real one, please?" The King asked.

'Yes, your majesty. If you bite a real Stater, it should leave bite marks along the edge.'

"I would like to bite a coin. You may approach my throne." He approached the throne and gave The King the fake coin first. The King bit into it and he spat out gold paint. Then he bit into the second coin and looked at the edge; there were teeth marks on it.

"What was your plan for the coins?" The King asked.

"Nadal had commissioned me to make them. The Vizier had planned to steal all the money in circulation and replace it with my forgeries. Nadal wanted Tarnuz to go bankrupt. He thought that if other countries knew about our fake money, they would stop trading with us."

With a flash of green smoke Nadal had disappeared and then he reappeared at the palace doors, he smiled his sly smile and departed.

Tina ran after him. She skidded on the street as Nadal galloped away. She found a horse, and gave chase. The city flashed by and buildings became hills and hills became a forest. Nadal had dismounted and was standing in the clearing. He drank from a vial and he cackled as his feet disappeared then his legs, followed by his torso and last of all his head.

"You think you are so clever, don't you? You think you are the only one with Dyidian knowledge? I was a scholar long before you were born."

"Everything is twisted in your world Nadal, including your vision of the Dyidians. I think they were intelligent people who used knowledge to educate and enhance people's lives. I think you have lost all sight of that."

He cackled "Oh such a naïve little thing aren't you. You have no idea about such matters."

His voice came from behind her and she whirled around with her Nimchar, but he kicked her in her stomach and she fell backwards. He ran past her, making her hair move. She turned around again, and he charged, and she swiped at him. He yelped and swore. She had caught his arm. His blood was visible, but Nadal wasn't. The trail of blood led around the tree.

"You can't win. None of you can stop me. I am too powerful for all of you, even that wretched brother of mine. I shall rid the world of all of you."

With a swish, she felt a tear in her arm and she yelled. His invisible blade cut her. She opened a vial and poured it on the wound, and with a hiss, the wound healed.

She uncorked a vial of firefly and swallowed it.

She took another vial and her vision wobbled, like she was underwater and then she could she Nadal crouching by a bush.

"Yah," She yelled and struck him with an overhead blow slashing his cheek.

He spun around like a whirling dervish slashing her torso. When he faced her again, she threw her sword pining him to a tree. The tree wrapped its branches round his wrists and ankles like wooden snakes, and he dropped his sword. Horse's hooves thundered towards her. She turned and saw the two Kings and their guards.

"Guards, take my brother away he can join his friend Clepta in prison. Empty his pockets. He won't need his bag of tricks." The guards frisked him and led him away. More horse's arrived and Stinu, Ali and Vernu dismounted.

"I cannot thank you enough. You have saved my kingdom and your country."

"I am also very impressed with you all," King Khalid said. 'I will not declare war on your country because of your brave efforts and magnificent food. King Stefano and I will form a peaceful alliance and we will assist you in times of trouble. We will trade and live in harmony, thanks to you.'

"Your Royal Highness, King Khalid, I have a parting gift for you," Stinu said.

"Ah, what can it be, Admiral," The King said, excitedly, rubbing his hands together.

Stinu reached into his bag and pulled out the gold necklace with the large ruby in it.

Khalid's eyes went as large as banquet plates when he saw it. Stinu dangled it before the monarch, he grabbed at it, but Stinu pulled it away.

"If you promise to leave Tarnuz alone, you can have this as a token of peace."

"I will be honest with you Admiral, rubies are my absolute favourite and I am greedy for jewellery. You have my word."

You're just greedy full stop! Stinu thought, looking at the portly King.

"Good here you go," And he handed him the trinket. The King handled it like a very expensive Sorapis, looking at it with wide eyes and a sinister grin on his face.

Sweat dripped down Tina's neck as she stacked the last box. Despite feeling exhausted, the market stall looked good, but she never wanted to see another onion.

"So what will you wear?"

"To what?"

"Our knighthood, silly," Ali said.

"Oh, I'm sure I'll find something," Tina replied.

Stinu stepped down from his ladder and clapped the white chalk from his hands.

"There. That will do for now. At least until we get a proper sign, of course. Vernu, The King flatters you with your dish having his seal of approval."

"If the King likes it, it gets his approval. I like his idea of making the dish available to everyone."

"Mistress Valentina, I have something for you," Galaxio said handed her a paper tube. She took it and placed it on the cobblestones.

"Thank you. I'll look at it later."

"Come see the sign." Her Father said. He stepped aside.

SPICE TRADERS

It read.

"It has a certain ring to it, doesn't it," he said.

They all nodded and smiled.

THE END

The Spice Traders will return in Tournament of Tannur.

Printed in Great Britain
by Amazon